AUTUMN'S ANGEL

CB SAMET

Romancing the Spirit

Cover Art: GetCovers

Print ISBN: 978-1-950942-13-8

❀ Formatted with Vellum

PRAISE FOR CB SAMET

" A collection of well-executed … tales of love and ghosts."

— KIRKUS REVIEW (ON ROMANCING THE SPIRIT SERIES BOOKS 1-6)

Four-time award winning author

GRAY HORIZON: 2019 Readers' Favorite Bronze Winner in Thriller category

MASTERS FILE: 2018 Readers' Favorite Honorable Mention in Romantic Suspense category

THE AVANT CHAMPION ~RISING~: 2017 EVVY Award 2nd Place in Fantasy category and 2018 Great Southeastern Book Festival Honorable Mention in Fantasy

A ROMANCING THE
SPIRIT NOVELLA

AUTUMN'S ANGEL

CB SAMET

CHAPTER 1

*a*utumn Bentley's mark glanced over his shoulder before walking into a small building with a flashing neon sign:

DEVLIN'S PSYCHIC READINGS

Under the near-midday sun, the short, stocky Bernard Warden vanished from Autumn's view. Why would a smuggler go to a fortune-teller? Unless this place was a front for hiding stolen or fake goods.

The single story, brick rectangular structure had a gable roof. Outside the front door, carved pumpkins displayed their crooked smiles.

She needed to get her eyes and ears on the inside of that building, but she wouldn't learn anything by barging through the front door. Walking around back, she glanced around at the other commercial shops and tried to look inconspicuous in broad daylight.

Finding the back entrance, obscured by five-foot-tall summersweet bushes on either side, she tested the door-knob. Locked.

Bending down, she noticed the plants' late-summer blooms had withered and fallen to the ground as their leaves transformed to a vibrant yellow for the fall. With-drawing her lock pick, she set to work on the simple latch bolt on a rotating knob.

When the lock gave way, she eased herself inside a kitchenette. It had a small refrigerator, microwave, and a round, two-seater table. Following the sound of voices, Autumn crept down a hallway. Hanging purple beads glinted over an archway that led to a front room. She hugged one wall and squinted through the beads.

Bernard, Autumn's mark, sat at a round table deco-rated with a shimmering purple tablecloth, on top of which perched a clear orb. Across the table from Bernard sat a gray-bearded man in a cheap black tuxedo. He wore an oversized black top hat as he hunched over, staring at tarot cards spread on the table. Was this man Devlin, the owner of DEVLIN'S PSYCHIC READINGS, or was Devlin a *nom de plume*?

The room had dark paneled walls, and thick purple drapes filtered sunlight down to a faint glow. Candles and incense smelling of cinnamon burned on a decorative stand against one wall.

Autumn frowned. She thought she would catch Bernard elbow deep in illicit activity, not doing a tarot card reading. There had to be more transpiring here than met the eye. Perhaps this silver-bearded charlatan ran a front for forged art.

She rolled her shoulders, feeling the weight of her Glock in its harness. She would discover the secret of this clandestine meeting, even if it meant eavesdropping throughout the entire preposterous psychic reading.

DEVLIN SHUFFLED the deck of tarot cards. His customer seated on the opposite side of the round table was a regular. Bernard visited Devlin once a month to commune with Joy, his deceased ex-wife. He'd initially come to see his grandmother, but Devlin could only see ghosts who hadn't crossed over yet. Spirits at rest couldn't be summoned. When Devlin tried for Bernard's grandmother, he'd received no reply.

Of Bernard's relatives, his ex-wife was the only one still lingering. So he came to speak with Joy monthly and have Devlin read his future. Devlin had explained that tarot cards weren't his strong suit and couldn't reliably predict the future, but Bernard came faithfully, paid faithfully, and listened with rapt attention. The interaction seemed to be helping both him and his ex-wife as they mended their relationship from across the grave, and Joy encouraged Bernard to become a better man.

Joy, a boisterous Southern belle in her fifties, had a great beehive of bleach blonde hair and an even bigger heart. She talked incessantly in a sticky-sweet Southern drawl, but Bernard only heard what Devlin filtered down to him.

As Devlin read the tarot cards, Joy floated nearby and observed her ex-husband's reaction. Devlin flipped the third card face up on the table—Death. He cleared his throat and scooped up the cards to reshuffle.

"What was that?"

"Nothing, sir. Let's do it again." Devlin masked his normal voice with a fake British accent. He was probably butchering the accent, but no one who came for psychic readings to a shack in Sacramento would be able to tell the difference.

After shuffling, Devlin turned over the top card—Death again.

"Death?" Bernard asked in a croak.

"Sometimes death is a new beginning." Devlin could hear his own voice losing the elderly tone and accented disguise as the hair on the back of his neck stood on end. He'd never had the Death card rear its ugly head.

The card didn't necessarily represent physical death. It often meant a change, such as a relationship or a career change. Yet, Devlin sensed doom as he touched a finger to the skeleton figure on the card.

Joy crossed her translucent arms. "Well, Lordy! Ain't that a hot mess. I reckon Bernard's gettin' the short end of the stick. He'll be joining me soon."

Devlin looked up at the bulbous spirit of Bernard's ex-wife. Joy had died of a heart attack a year ago, but she and Bernard had already been divorced for about five years. She'd divorced him when he'd refused to quit his illegal activities, after which she remarried and became Joy Porter.

"What's it mean?" Bernard asked. His expression of wide-eyed worry and his jutting jaw had him looking like a spooked filly.

Joy's transparent face looked solemn. "Honey, that's as ominous as dark clouds before a hurricane. Somethin' gawd-awful is about to put his knickers in a knot."

The front door burst open. A tall thin figure, who might have been a skeleton of Death himself, stood haloed in light from the midday sun. The man raised a gun and fired.

AUTUMN HEARD the splintering of wood as someone kicked in the front door. A lanky man fired two successive shots aimed at Bernard.

Bernard fell back in his chair, landing on the floor with a thud. Simultaneously, the fortune-teller dove behind the table, his hat flying off his head.

As Autumn pulled her Glock, she shouted, "FBI! Freeze!"

The gunman wasted no time in firing his weapon at Autumn. She quickly crouched back behind the wall, but as the bullets punctured the thin plaster walls, Autumn realized she didn't have much cover. She counted the number of bullets fired as splinters flew around her. She'd glimpsed the assailant's Ruger SR22. At most, he had ten bullets before he'd have to reload.

After the tenth round, she leapt up and pressed through the beads hanging in the archway, prepared to return fire. But the figure had vanished.

Heart pounding, Autumn surveyed the scene as she cautiously passed through the room with gun raised. Bernard lay sprawled on the floor with the other man—presumably the psychic reader, Devlin—kneeling over him. Autumn couldn't be sure if Devlin had been injured as well.

"Stay down!" she barked.

When Autumn reached the doorway, she cautiously scanned the perimeter. The sound of a car engine caught her attention. She sprinted after it. As she slowed and took aim at the front tire, the driver-side window lowered.

"Crap!" She dove to the side and rolled onto the lawn as the gunman fired again. Behind her, one of the pumpkins erupted. By the time Autumn tumbled and sprang to her feet, the car had swerved onto the main road and accelerated away from her.

Holstering her gun, Autumn swore. She shook out an ache in her left arm. She must have jarred something when she rolled. She walked back into Devlin's lair and pulled out her phone.

"9-1-1. What's your emergency?"

"Gunshot victim." Autumn gave the address as she looked down at Bernard, lying in a pool of his own blood.

Devlin, who was surprisingly not shrieking in terror at the shootout and man bleeding on his purple carpet, was administering first aid. He'd stripped his table of the purple cloth and applied pressure to Bernard's chest wound.

With EMS activated, Autumn disconnected the call and took a steadying breath. The police would arrive soon, and she didn't have time for local PD stalling her case. But she couldn't leave the scene of a crime. At the very least, she needed to get information from this charlatan before the police took him out of her reach.

"What did Bernard say to you before he was shot?"

"What?" Devlin sounded breathless from his effort.

"You were talking to Bernard before the hitman arrived. What were you talking about?"

"How to make cherry pie," he snapped.

"What?"

He glared up at her. "I'm a medium. What do you think we were talking about?"

Autumn narrowed her eyes and knelt down beside him, careful not to interfere with his first-aid efforts. Devlin's voice sounded all wrong. His wasn't the voice of an old British aristocrat—not as it had been earlier. He sounded young and American. With his hat off, disheveled dark-brown hair was visible. She scrutinized the silver strands of hair jutting off the man's chin—coarse, synthetic hair. If Autumn had one gift, it was how to spot a fake.

She tugged off the fake beard, revealing a handsome face and green eyes on a man who looked to be about thirty-five.

"Do you mind?" he snapped. A young Devlin rocked back on his heels and wiped the blood from his hands onto the tablecloth.

"Are you injured?" she asked him.

He stared at Bernard, who gazed lifelessly at the ceiling.

Autumn snapped her fingers close to Devlin's face. "Hey! Cherry Pie! Are you injured?"

"No. But Bernard is dead."

"Should we do CPR?"

Devlin turned his blazing green eyes in her direction.

"Cardiopulmonary resuscitation requires a functioning cardiopulmonary circuit. He no longer has one. He doesn't have any blood left to circulate. He's dead." Devlin turned away from her and appeared to be speaking to Bernard. "I'm sorry."

"I need to know your relationship with this man and everything he's told you."

The magician blinked at her. "Why?"

"He's part of an FBI investigation."

"Can I see some ID?"

Autumn obliged, showing him her credentials as Agent Bentley of the FBI from her wallet before tucking it back in her jacket pocket.

The man nodded and looked up at her. The hat had disheveled his hair. He turned his sad gaze back to Bernard briefly before looking at Autumn again, this time with panicked worry in his expression.

"You called 9-1-1."

Autumn arched an eyebrow. "Most people do when someone's been shot."

Devlin stood and placed a finger to his temple. "I can't be here when the police get here."

His alarm surprised her, but he seemed afraid and not dangerous.

"Are you wanted for something?" she asked.

The accusatory tone of her voice had his eyes narrowing, and he took a step back. She held his gaze, waiting for an answer.

Devlin turned, hastening toward the kitchenette. "I have to go." He shrugged out of his penguin jacket.

"You're not leaving the crime scene. And I need to see some identification."

Who was this man pretending to be an old psychic, and why was he so fearful of the police? Autumn exposed frauds constantly in her job, and she would expose this one, too, good looks aside.

CHAPTER 2

*D*evlin scrubbed the blood off his hands and fingernails. He'd thought he'd never have to do this again. He'd been wrong.

Picking up his briefcase from the counter, he stepped out of his suede dress shoes, and slipped on his black Oxfords. He absolutely couldn't be here when the police arrived.

Joy sobbed loudly in the other room over Bernard's body. Devlin may not have answers as to what Bernard had done that bought him two bullets to the chest, but he knew who might have answers.

Devlin dumped his crystal ball and tarot cards into his briefcase, aware of Special Agent Bentley's grinding glare.

"Look, Cherry Pie." Her voice had grown a sharp edge. "If you don't start talking, I'm going to restrain you."

Devlin believed her slim five-foot-six figure was fully capable of restraining him, and he didn't think it'd be wholly unpleasant. His eyes roamed Autumn's physique beneath the navy suit she wore. Her skin shone a smooth cream color around wide, full lips. Long, loose, dark-brown hair was woven with strands of gold and auburn.

He might have been intimidated by her authoritative presence if he hadn't already been so familiar with fear and running and law enforcement.

"Get me out of here, Agent Bentley, and I'll tell you everything I can."

She slitted her golden eyes, but she didn't say no.

Devlin glanced at Joy, who wiped at nonexistent tears as she hovered above Bernard. Joy would have the information Autumn sought—at least some of it—but Devlin couldn't start carrying on a conversation with Joy in front of the FBI agent. Instead, he gave the ghost a pleading look.

Joy sniffed. "Lordy, I need a stiff whiskey bourbon. Your FBI woman is after Bernard's forged art. Except it ain't art."

Devlin had no idea what Joy was referring to, but he decided to use it to his advantage, anyway. "I'll tell you about the forged art."

Autumn's jaw tensed, and mistrust flooded her golden eyes, turning them amber. He decidedly didn't like the judgment in her beautiful features—oval face, tapered nose, and soft cheekbones. He wasn't involved in anything illegal, but there'd be no convincing the FBI agent of that now.

"Let's go," she said with a growl.

As he turned, he noticed a tear in Autumn's suit jacket with an unmistakable dark stain of blood. "You've been shot."

Autumn glanced down at the blood as if noticing it for the first time. "I'll check it in the car."

They exited the back door, and he walked toward his car. Autumn eyed Devlin's blue Prius as he unlocked the car remotely.

"I'm parked down the road," she said, as if expecting him to change course toward her car.

"Well, mine's closer. Or you could follow me." No way she'd accept that offer, he suspected.

"The hitman may know your license plate or may have planted something in your car. We're taking mine."

"Fine," he huffed. He dragged out Kimmy's booster seat before following Autumn down the drive. Glancing left and right, he was keenly aware of gawkers who had emerged from other businesses on either side of his, presumably drawn by the sound of gunshots.

He kept pace with Autumn's long, quick strides.

"What is that for?" she asked, nodding at the car seat.

"My daughter. We need to pick her up from school."

Autumn unlocked her navy Acura TLX before staring incredulously at Devlin. He ignored the twitching of her right eye as he shoved the seat in the back and tossed his briefcase on the floor. She climbed into the driver's seat and tugged on her seatbelt.

"Your daughter?" She started the car.

"She's in first grade."

"We aren't picking up any kids until I get some answers." She pulled away from the curb.

"Bernard's death is going to expose me, so Kimmy gets to safety first." Touching the console, Devlin set the car's GPS destination to Kimmy's school.

Autumn scowled. "The premise for leaving the crime scene was that you needed to leave the building."

"Yes, and that includes picking up my daughter."

"Start talking."

Joy materialized in the back seat, still quietly sobbing. "He looks like a dozen miles of bad road. We're just going to leave him there? My poor sweet Bernard. Bless his heart."

Poor sweet Bernard had hurtled Devlin's life into a world of chaos. *Back* into a world of chaos. He'd spent six years rebuilding a life—carefully, meticulously—and now it was shattered shards of glass, exposing him to jagged danger all over again.

"I'm sorry," he told Joy.

Autumn took a left, following the automated voice's directions. "I don't want an apology. I want an explanation."

Devlin shook his head. Of course she'd assumed he was talking to her.

She continued, "I want to know the nature of your relationship with Bernard and who shot him. I want to know why he was shot and who his buyer is for the forged art."

Devlin didn't know the answers to any of Autumn's inquiries, but he had a resource who might. If Joy didn't already know what Bernard was involved in from their years of marriage, she might be able to find out. Ghosts could glean information about people—sometimes general knowledge, sometimes secrets.

He didn't need Joy to tell him every minute detail about Bernard's illicit dealings, just enough to get Agent

Bentley on a trail that wasn't Devlin's. The sooner he rid himself of her and this art forging scandal, the sooner he could hide in safety... again.

His gut clenched when two police cars raced past them, heading in the opposite direction. He glanced to the back seat, where Joy was in no condition to discuss Bernard's dirty deeds.

"Okay." Autumn took a deep breath. "Let's at least start with a name."

Joy didn't volunteer any information.

"I don't know who the shooter was."

"Your name." Autumn ran a frustrated hand through her hair.

Devlin suspected most men saw those thick, dark waves of hair and those golden eyes and confessed all sorts of things. Devlin wasn't most men, and he'd expended too much hard work to get where he was to throw it away in a lustful confession.

"Cherry Pie seems to work." *What's in a name?* He'd have to change it again anyway after this debacle. Too bad. He liked Devlin Angelo. It had an edge to it.

Autumn drew in a breath, no doubt about to unleash her authoritative voice again, when Devlin reached up and gently removed a dry leaf from her hair.

With lightning reflexes, she caught his hand with the leaf in his fingers and inspected it. Her hard expression softened, but Devlin couldn't associate an emotion with it. She turned her attention back to the road and slowly released his hand. Her touch left a lingering sensation on his skin.

"You have more on your jacket and in your hair."

Devlin turned to stare out the front window at the road. "My name is Devlin Angelo."

Autumn pursed her lips. "And why is Bernard dead? And why was I shot at?"

Devlin glanced at Joy again to see the ghost had her face buried in her hands.

"It might take time to extract the information." He gave Autumn a sheepish grin.

"What does that even mean? This isn't drawing sap from a tree. Just tell me what you know."

"I'm more clueless than you about why someone shot Bernard, but I know someone who might know."

Autumn threw a hand up in frustration and then grimaced. She pursed her lips as her cheeks flared red. "I don't know what game you're playing, but you are not an innocent bystander, and I will get to the bottom of this."

"No games."

But Autumn was correct about Devlin not being innocent. Innocence had not been a term in his vocabulary in years, unless he was referring to Kimmy.

Autumn's complexion paled slightly.

"Are you okay?"

"My arm's throbbing. I think the wound had clotted and now it's bleeding again. Can you grab the pad out of the glove compartment?"

Devlin obliged.

"Unwrap it and shove it under my jacket sleeve."

He gave her a speculative look.

"Please," she added.

He unwrapped the pad as Autumn shrugged one shoulder out of her blazer, keeping her other hand on the wheel. Devlin tucked the pad against her inside, absorbent side to her arm and sticky side to the inside of her jacket sleeve. The snug fit and adhesive would keep it in place. When he finished, he helped pull her blazer back over her shoulder.

"I need to make a phone call," he said.

"To whom?" Autumn asked.

"US Marshal Harriet Williams."

"You have the US Marshal on speed dial?"

"For emergencies, yes."

Autumn pulled out her phone. "I'll call."

Devlin rattled off the number.

Autumn dialed the number as her temper rippled through her in waves of heat. A man was dead. Autumn had left the scene of the crime. She'd been shot. Now, she was driving with a man who posed as a psychic, remained calm in a shooting, had a contact at the US Marshals office, and had a daughter.

None of this made sense, and Devlin wasn't forthcoming. Perhaps she could get information from the US Marshal.

A gruff female voice answered the phone. "Williams."

"This is Special Agent Bentley of the FBI. I'm with Devlin Angelo, who says he knows you."

"Is he injured?" the US Marshal asked, the gravel in her voice growing an edge of worry.

"Aside from being neck-deep in a homicide, he's a picture of health."

Autumn glanced at Devlin long enough to see the

corner of his mouth curl before she looked back to the road.

"Homicide? Are you implying he's the culprit?"

"No. But I need some answers."

"Is he in danger right now?"

Autumn had been watching for a tail, and they weren't being followed. She glanced at Devlin, who swallowed hard. He was afraid, she realized. His hands fidgeted with a tarot card as they drove to his daughter's school.

"No. Is there a reason he'd be in danger?"

"What has he told you?"

"Not a damn thing."

"Well, I'm not debriefing an agent I've never met over the phone. We'll meet and talk with Devlin. Present and unharmed."

Autumn bristled. Devlin wasn't in danger from her. She held out the phone to Devlin. "Can you please assure the US Marshal that you're unharmed and I pose no threat to you?"

"Well, you did threaten to restrain me."

The quirk of his lips, twinkle in his eyes, and frame of dark hair looked intriguingly playful. And gave her an unfamiliar sensation of butterflies in her stomach.

She gave Devlin a stern arched brow, but rather than force him into submission, her expression made him smile. She scowled. She was an excellent interrogator and had solved cases by intimidating thieves with that look, but her technique flowed around Devlin like a river parted by a stone.

"I'm fine, Harriet," Devlin said loudly. "This isn't my mess, and it isn't related to Oscar."

Autumn pulled the phone back to her ear. "Is meeting feasible? Where are you stationed?"

"Devlin knows where to meet. Motel. One hour."

When Harriet disconnected the call, Autumn put her phone back in her jacket pocket.

"What did she say?" Devlin asked.

"That I'm one hundred percent trustworthy, and you need to fully cooperate with questioning."

"Ha! A for effort though, Special Agent Bentley."

Autumn grinned as she realized how infectious Devlin's smile was. "She said you'd know where to meet."

Devlin pursed his lips and nodded.

"Who's Oscar?" she asked.

Devlin's face drained of color and his green eyes darkened, but he didn't answer her question.

Following GPS directions, she took a left and pulled into the parking lot of an elementary school.

"I'll be right back." Devlin reached for the door handle.

Autumn placed a hand on his shoulder before he could dash out of the car. "I'm coming with you."

His eyes grazed her with heated frustration. He would rightly assume she didn't trust him after how he'd behaved, but she also had his safety in mind. Something had Devlin racing to pick up his daughter. Someone named Oscar invoked more fear in him than a hitman in action, and some danger in his life had a US Marshal worried about his safety.

Autumn closed her jacket over her concealed weapon and walked beside Devlin into the school. She waited with him as the front desk assistant fetched Kimmy from her classroom.

Devlin absently turned a tarot card through his fingers as they waited.

"Daddy!" A small girl with thick, dark hair in a pony-tail leaped into her father's arms.

He hugged her and spun her in a circle. In one hand, she clutched a pink nylon lunch bag and in the other a rolled piece of paper.

"Kimmy." Devlin embraced her until the girl squirmed free.

Kimmy thrust the paper at her father, beaming. "I wrote the alphabet."

Devlin stood and opened the paper. "You sure did. And so neat, too."

Kimmy smiled at the compliment before turning her inquisitive green eyes on Autumn. "Who's she?"

Autumn bent down. "Autumn Bentley."

"Daddy, did you make a new friend?" Her small voice filled with astonishment.

Devlin looked back and forth from Autumn to Kimmy and back to Autumn. "I have friends," he said defensively, stretching taller.

Kimmy looked up at her father as if he'd claimed to have sprouted wings.

When Autumn smiled, Kimmy took her hand, and they walked toward the exit. "I like the name Autumn. Our last name has an A, too. It's Angelo. A girl in my class is named Angela. She's angel with an *a* and daddy's angel with an *o*. It's okay. Boys can be angels, too."

Autumn led Kimmy toward her rental car as a speech-less Devlin trailed behind them. "My Sunday school teacher taught us about angels. There's Gabriel and

Michael and…" Kimmy rattled off a half dozen more as Autumn opened the back door for her.

"Why do you have a gun?"

Autumn glanced down to see that her jacket had opened, and her Glock was visible as she leaned over to help Kimmy with the seatbelt.

"To help me catch bad guys."

Kimmy's mouth made an *O* shape. "So you help people too, like an angel?"

Autumn coughed. Never had she thought of herself as an angel.

"Did you catch any bad guys today?" the girl asked.

"No." Autumn sighed. "He got away, but the day is still young." She glanced at Devlin before closing the door. After climbing into the driver's seat, she started the car.

Kimmy continued, "That's okay. Even in movies, sometimes the bad guys get away. Daddy says sometimes bad guys make people move when they don't want to. It's Halloween today. I'm going to be Wonder Woman. Do you have a costume? You could be Wonder Woman too since you catch bad guys."

Beside her, Devlin grimaced. "Kimmy, we're going to see Harriet. Do you want to stop for a snack on the way?"

Sometimes bad guys make people move… make people relocate and change identities. Damn. And Devlin's handler in the Witness Security Program was US Marshal Harriet Williams.

Pieces were falling into place.

Autumn stole another look at Devlin as he talked with Kimmy. Many of the people in WITSEC were criminals themselves—they just ratted out bigger fish. So, Devlin had a checkered past, and now he was tangled up in a homicide investigation. Autumn had a thousand questions for him, but she couldn't interrogate him in front of his six-year-old daughter.

Autumn wasn't Wonder Woman.

Devlin was a mystery.

And who was Oscar?

CHAPTER 3

*A*s they drove to the motel to meet Harriet, Devlin felt the familiar corset of angst loosen from around his chest. Kimmy sat safely in the car with him, and her six-year-old chatter soothed the lingering ache of worry.

Autumn seemed surprisingly at ease in Kimmy's presence and perhaps even a little smitten with her charm. Not that it mattered. Everyone Kimmy knew today would be out of their lives tomorrow.

Spirits save me.

Would he have to assign Kimmy a new name, too? Would Harriet stay his handler if they had to move to a new state?

And they would have to move. The police investigation into Bernard's death and whatever investigation Autumn led the FBI through would lead to documentation. Documentation that could be traced and tracked back to him. And then Oscar would find them.

"Daddy, can I do screens?"

The question reminded Devlin that he needed to remove his SIM card. The drive to the motel would take another ten minutes. He could wait ten more minutes. Devlin rooted in his pocket and passed his phone to Kimmy.

Joy hovered beside Kimmy, looking sullen and shimmering in the afternoon light streaming through her body. Fortunately, Kimmy couldn't see ghosts.

Devlin turned to Autumn. "Can we stop at a convenience store so I can buy Kimmy a snack?"

Autumn obliged, pulling into the parking lot of a drugstore and grabbing a spot near the entrance. He made a quick trip for peanut butter crackers, water, and a first aid kit. Soon, they were back on the road.

Devlin pondered his next identity as he twirled a tarot card in his hands. He couldn't be a psychic reader in his next life. He missed being a paramedic. Maybe he could befriend a ghost who could school him in finance. Whatever it took to keep Kimmy safe.

"Are you okay?" Autumn asked.

Devlin stopped flipping the card. It was probably annoying to someone who didn't understand his predicament. "Not really. And I'm honestly not trying to be difficult."

"You're protecting Kimmy. I get that."

Devlin lowered his voice. "I will get you whatever answers I can, but not... "

"In front of your daughter. That's fine."

The car seemed to drift in silence for several heartbeats, except for the music of the game Kimmy played on Devlin's phone.

"WITSEC?"

Devlin ran a hand through his hair before rubbing his neck.

"When was the last relocation?"

"When Kimmy was born. That's when I—we—entered."

Autumn nodded. She looked like she had a dozen more questions behind her amber, calculating eyes, but she didn't ask, didn't press. Devlin felt grateful—he didn't want her interrogating him, even in a calm tone, in front of Kimmy.

Autumn pulled into the motel parking lot where they planned to meet Harriet. Outside the lobby, Halloween pumpkins squatted beside orange chrysanthemums.

"This is the meeting place?"

Devlin nodded, flipping the card through his fingers once more. "I go in, rent a room, and pay cash under the name Sam Sampson."

"I'll get the room, so you won't be seen." Pulling out her phone, she kept her voice low to Devlin. "I need to let my boss know about the shooting." She put a hand up as he started to open his mouth. "I won't share anything about you... yet."

Devlin's heart rate had ratcheted up at the thought of Autumn alerting the FBI. Investigation. Digging. Accessible information for someone connected to powerful people—like Oscar.

"Devlin?" Autumn looked at him expectantly.

Had she said something? He'd missed it.

"You'll stay here?" she asked.

Devlin looked as she pocketed her keys. No way to expeditiously run away. He nodded.

Autumn still stared at him, so he held her gaze to convey the truth of his agreement to stay. Her intense expression made her look like the steadfast law-woman she was. Devlin felt inclined to trust her, and he rarely trusted the living.

Ghosts he trusted. Ghosts didn't cheat, steal, or murder. Maybe he could trust Autumn, too. Maybe she'd trust him. The thought of Kimmy calling him an angel made Devlin smile.

Autumn opened the door and exited the car. As she walked away, he imagined her in a Halloween Wonder Woman costume. She certainly seemed to fit the part—steadfast, reliable, and out for justice. If she hadn't returned fire in his office, he wouldn't have had time to dive for cover under the table and might have been shot simply for being a witness to Bernard's assassination.

She'd saved his life. In exchange, the very least he could do was coax Joy into divulging whatever she could about Bernard's crooked deeds. Forged art that wasn't art. Meaning what exactly? Once secrets were spilled, Autumn and Devlin would be square. Debt repaid.

If he'd learned anything from ghosts, it was to never let the sun set on unfinished business. Life was short and could end at any moment. Regrets, debts, and unreconciled emotional turmoil could all pin a spirit to this world. He tried not to accumulate these things. And what of regretting the events that had put him into witness protection? He couldn't change those events either, but he and Kimmy had survived them.

When Autumn disappeared inside the motel, Devlin turned in his seat. The contents of his briefcase had jostled during the car ride and spilled onto the floor back there.

"Hey, Kimmy, did you have a good day at school?"

His daughter smiled but didn't look up from her game. Usually Devlin spent the drive home talking with her, but today, distraction was better under the circumstances. Devlin wanted her to remain unaware of any potential danger.

Joy still sat beside her in the car. Devlin diligently tried to avoid talking to ghosts when he was around Kimmy. He didn't need the child telling a teacher her father talked to himself. If Kimmy turned out to be anything like Devlin or Devlin's mother, then she would develop the gift around age sixteen. But Devlin's mother had warned him that becoming a medium could occur at any age.

Most of the ghosts Devlin had met were troubled souls seeking closure. Most were harmless and sometimes chatty, like Joy. None were dangerous or villainous or even particularly scary.

He fidgeted with the card in his hand, wanting to ask Joy about Bernard's dealings so he had something to offer Agent Bentley. But not in front of Kimmy. Devlin had only ever told one person about his gift, and she wasn't alive any longer.

CHAPTER 4

*a*fter checking in to the motel, Autumn lingered outside the lobby, discussing the homicide with her boss while keeping line of sight on her car. She explained that she currently had one lead pending on the forgery case, but she omitted Devlin's name.

Now that Autumn knew he was in WITSEC, she'd started to give him the benefit of the doubt. Perhaps he wasn't involved in the forgery or Bernard's death. She struggled to believe anyone who went through the trouble of relocating and changing their identity—especially with a child—would do anything to jeopardize that new life.

After she'd hung up the phone with her superior, she climbed back in the car and drove to the room, parking three spaces down from the assigned door marked twenty-one. She texted Marshal Williams the number.

Devlin followed her into the room, carrying his briefcase and grocery bag, with Kimmy marching between them. Once inside, he fed Kimmy peanut butter crackers, trail nuts, and water. After a few minutes of coaxing, he convinced her to take a nap before US Marshal Williams arrived.

When Devlin turned toward Autumn, she gave him an expectant look. She'd been more than patient and was ready for answers. Devlin picked up his plastic drugstore bag and motioned for her to come with him into the bathroom.

He quietly eased the door shut once she stood inside with him. The small space wouldn't allow two people to move without bumping into one another.

Devlin pulled a firstaid kit from the bag and opened it on the counter. Autumn took his cue and began tugging off her jacket. She took off the pad that had been used to absorb the bleeding earlier.

"You're going to need to take off your shirt, too."

She looked down at the dried blood and tear in her white collared shirt.

"It's okay. I'm a paramedic, or at least, I was a paramedic."

"The sleeve will roll up. I don't care if it's tight. I'm not removing my shirt."

"Suit yourself."

When she'd finished tugging off her jacket, his eyes grew momentarily heavy-lidded, and he hesitated. Paramedic or not, he apparently found her attractive. The feeling was mutual, though she wouldn't act on it. Autumn had a case to solve, and Devlin was a stranger with a new life to build. She tucked strands of hair behind her ear as he rolled up her shirtsleeve high enough to reveal the wound.

"You're lucky it's just a graze." He pulled disinfectant

out of the medical kit.

She watched the emerald glow of his eyes behind dark lashes and the small parting of his lips as he focused on his task.

When he applied the wound cleanser, she hissed. "That stung more than getting shot."

"That's because you had adrenaline working in your favor. Don't worry. I've taken care of grown men with smaller injuries than this who cried. Your vulnerability is safe with me."

"I'm not going to cry." She adjusted her gun holster.

"I wouldn't judge you if you did. I'd probably bawl like a baby if I'd been shot." His voice hitched at the end of his sentence. "You saved my life, you know."

"The thought crossed my mind." She grinned at him, trying to dispel his unease. "But you had wits enough to dive for cover."

She extended her hands, noting the slight tremor in them before moving them to grip the edge of the counter.

"First time getting shot?" he asked.

"Yes."

"First time shooting at someone else?"

"No."

He inspected the wound, delicate fingers touching her bare skin. He rotated her arm to catch the light from different angles. "It's not deep."

"I'll live?"

He gave her a wry grin. "No stitches, but you'll have a gouged-looking scar."

He pulled bandages out of the pack before clearing his throat. "There are a few ways we can do this. The best way for *me* to get answers for you is if you to leave me alone in the bathroom, talking to myself."

She watched him lay down a four-by-four pad over her graze and begin wrapping her arm with gauze.

He continued. "The best way for *you* to get the answers you want is to stay and have a three-way conversation with a spirit friend." He pursed his lips and avoided eye contact. "Either way, you'll think I'm crazy and doubt whatever information I get for you."

"A three-way conversation?" Already, a bathroom interrogation and a homicide were new and unusual events for her. She dealt with white-collar criminals, not violent offenders. Why not add a three-way conversation between two people to her list of bizarre activities for the day? "What does that mean?"

"Joy Porter is Bernard's ex-wife." He taped the bandage down over Autumn's arm.

"Yes," she agreed. "She died a year ago. Heart attack." Autumn pulled her jacket on and felt surprised to see a slight frown of dissatisfaction on Devlin's face. Was he disappointed she knew about Joy or disappointed she was dressing?

"Yes, and Bernard came to me to commune with his grandmother, but Joy showed up instead. If a spirit has moved on, I can't summon them back."

"And what does any of this voodoo have to do with my answers?"

Did he really believe he was a psychic?

Devlin began carefully packing supplies back in the first aid kit and discarding wrappers. "Joy is here with us, and, despite her grieving, I think she'll be willing to answer your questions if it means helping solve the mystery of Bernard's death."

Autumn shifted her weight. "You're honestly going to try to sell me a seance in a motel bathroom? Look, Mr. Angelo, I didn't hand you in for questioning or feed you to the police, *and* I let you pick up your little girl. You owe me answers." Was this some type of Halloween joke? After all, it was October thirty-first, and she was in a motel room with a man claiming to speak to ghosts.

"And I want to give you the answers you need. I honestly don't know what's going on, but Joy might." Devlin's tone had turned pleading.

"Absurd. Even if I believed you about the ghost, how would his dead *ex*-wife know anything?"

"Ghosts can glean information. For instance, Joy knows that you rose to the top of your class in the academy and you wanted to do art forgery because your fiancé's parents own an art gallery." Devlin glanced from her to a space above her on the cream-colored wall.

Autumn blinked at Devlin, at first stunned, and then wondering if this was part of the parlor trick.

"Oh. Ex-fiancé. He broke things off. Sorry." Casting his eyes down, Devlin zipped shut the first aid kit.

Autumn felt her temple throb.

"Joy, how about sharing what you know about Bernard's activities?" Devlin asked.

Handsome and crazy, Autumn thought. Yet, she had no choice but to hear Devlin out for several reasons. Unfortunately, she had to wait until the US Marshal arrived, because she'd promised to deliver Devlin safely. Plus, there was a sleeping six-year-old on the other side of the bathroom door. And she really had no leads on her case since Bernard was dead.

Devlin appeared to be listening to someone. He put one hand on his hip while the other rested on the counter near Autumn.

He turned an earnest gaze to Autumn. "So, Joy tells me that Bernard's a middleman—a courier. He's always been the mover of goods, usually either stolen or illegal drugs. Forged art is new for him, apparently, but it doesn't surprise Joy." Devlin turned back to where Joy supposedly sat—or hovered or floated or whatever. "I know. I'm sorry." He turned back to Autumn. "Anyway, Bernard wouldn't have been the actual forger, just the delivery man." His eyes cut right then back to Autumn. "A competent, reliable delivery man."

"I know all of this," Autumn said.

Suddenly, Devlin was looking less innocent and more involved by the second.

Devlin shifted his weight, unintentionally bumping his thigh into hers. "Well, I didn't know any of that. So, why don't you ask what you would ask Bernard if he was alive? We'll see if Joy knows the answer. And," he pointed a finger at her, "you can stop glaring at me like I'm a criminal."

Autumn grinned at his cuteness despite herself. "Who is your buyer?"

"Bernard's buyer. Who is Bernard's buyer?" Devlin restated the question. He cocked his head to one side, listening.

Autumn, all the while, was acutely aware of how close they stood together in the bathroom. This close, she could see fine wrinkles around his eyes from smiling. She wondered if Kimmy had put those there. She also noted Devlin wore no ring and had mentioned nothing about Kimmy's mother.

"No buyers. He was contracted to move the paintings across the border."

"Contracted by whom?"

"Cesar Torres?"

Was he asking her? No, she decided, the inflection was to see if the name resonated to her on some level. It didn't. She knew black-market art dealers, and Cesar Torres wasn't one of them.

"So, Cesar is moving fake art across the Mexican border?"

She ran both hands through her hair and shook out any remaining leaves from the dive she'd made in Devlin's lawn. She grimaced at the pain in her arm from the motion.

Devlin pulled a leaf that had fallen onto her jacket before moving his hands to straighten her shirt collar. She could smell a hint of the spicy incense from his psychic reading room still on him. She stopped his hands. She didn't need his proximity clouding her judgment.

"To whom is Cesar Torres selling the art?"

"Joy doesn't know." Devlin took a step back, and she released his hands.

Autumn studied Devlin's earnest face and bright eyes. Was this an act? He wasn't making a show of it—no eyes rolling back or voice changing an octave as he connected with the "spirit." There was nothing showy about his performance.

"Joy, please. I don't need to know that."

"Need to know what?" Autumn asked.

"Nothing."

"Devlin." She leveled a gaze at him.

"Your fiancé broke your heart." Devlin blew out a breath. "And took your dog?"

Devlin's expression of compassion for her loss curbed her initial reaction to be angry with him.

"How could you possibly know about Buster? And he was *our* dog. The decision was mutual. I travel a lot with work, which is unfair to a pet."

Devlin placed a hand on hers. "I can't control what information the spirits volunteer. I'm sorry. I didn't mean to learn personal information."

"So, let's make it even. Who's Oscar?"

As he withdrew his hand, Devlin's jaw hardened. Straightening, he squared his shoulders. "You, Agent Bentley, don't get to know that information without express permission from the US Marshals' office."

A knock sounded at the door, and Devlin startled. The motion had his legs brushing Autumn's again.

"It's Harriet." Devlin's voice sounded slightly breathless.

Autumn scrutinized his expression. If he was a lying, thieving criminal with an FBI agent on one side and a US Marshal on the other, he ought to be afraid, but he didn't appear to be.

Devlin exited the bathroom and walked toward the door, but Autumn quickened her pace and reached it before him.

"I'll check first." With one hand on her weapon, she asked, "Who is it?"

"US Marshal Williams. Devlin, are you okay?"

"Yes, I'm fine, and Kimmy's with me, napping."

"Can I talk to something other than a door?"

When Autumn opened the door, she saw a broad-shouldered woman sucking on a Camel cigarette. She wore jeans and a gray T-shirt.

"You must be Agent Bentley."

"Call me Autumn." She extended a hand.

Harriet shook it with a meaty, stern grip as she took one last drag on her cigarette. She stomped the butt under a thick-soled working boot before picking it up and tucking it into a pocket. "Suppose we should talk out here if the runt's still sleeping."

Autumn and Devlin stepped outside the motel room. As Autumn pulled the motel door shut, Devlin hugged Harriet.

The US Marshal gave him an awkward pat on the back. "Okay. Okay. You're safe, and I've got a reputation to uphold."

Devlin lingered a second longer. "Thank you for coming." He took a step back from Harriet. "Does this mean relocating us again?"

Harriet squinted, though no direct sunlight shone in her eyes. "Don't know yet. Let's talk to the local po-po before they start a manhunt and see how this plays out. Tell me what happened."

"Bernard Warden came to my office to commune with his ex-wife. He's a regular. He also likes card readings, so I started with the tarot deck. After the Death card came up, a shooter burst through the door and killed him. The gunman took aim at me when Special Agent Bentley caught his attention. She appeared out of nowhere. I dove for cover while Bernard's killer shot at her. There was no saving Bernard. The gunman fled. When we left the scene, Special Agent Bentley agreed to let me pick up Kimmy and call you in exchange for information."

"What information?" Harriet asked.

Devlin glanced at Autumn. "Special Agent Bentley specializes in cases of art forgery, and Bernard was her lead. Bernard's deceased ex-wife has been kind enough to share her information, even while grieving."

Harriet nudged Autumn's elbow. "The ghost thing's cool. Am I right?"

Autumn frowned and crossed her arms.

Harriet shrugged. "I didn't believe it at first. And then we did this whole session with my mother, who died twenty years ago. We worked through a lot of unresolved issues that day. Did Devlin show you the crystal ball?"

Autumn recalled Devlin putting an orb into his brief-case, but he hadn't pulled it back out again. "Crystal ball?"

"It's cool." Harriet wriggled her eyebrows. "It'll give you goosebumps."

Devlin shook his head. "She already thinks I'm crazy, Harriet. I'm not sure you're helping."

Harriet snorted. "If she sees the crystal ball, she'll be a believer."

"It doesn't work for everyone," Devlin said.

Autumn interrupted. "The only crystal ball I'm interested in is the one that helps me find this forged art."

Harriet pulled out her pack of cigarettes and tapped

the flat bottom against her palm. "Apparently, Special Agent Uptight doesn't have time for our shenanigans." She turned to Devlin. "Does she have what she needs to know? I need to get you in and out of police questioning."

"I have a lot of unanswered questions," Autumn said.

Harriet put the cigarette between her lips but didn't light it. "Well, you get three more, and then we're done here."

Autumn turned to Devlin. "Who is making the forged art?"

CHAPTER 5

 evlin turned to Joy, who hovered nearby.

"I've been channeling for you while you're playing dreamy-eyes with the agent. I've been as busy as a one-legged cat in a sandbox. Turns out. No one's creatin' art," Joy said.

"What does that mean?" Devlin asked.

"The art is printed and then pressed onto the canvas."

"Well, then it would obviously be fake, right? Those can't be worth anything."

"I don't know, darling," Joy squeaked, distraught. "I wasn't around him for the last year, so I don't know what all Bernard's been up to. He took any paying job that kept the porch light on. I can't make sense of what I see. Stop rufflin' my feathers." Her intonation began to reach the pitch of a wail. She fanned herself in agitation, her blonde updo unwavering.

"Okay. It's okay. We'll figure it out. I appreciate your help."

Autumn cleared her throat.

"Joy says it's printed—not painted—on canvas."

Autumn shifted her weight irritably. "So there are horrendous fabrications crossing the border which no one is buying and to no purpose?" She pointed a finger at Harriet. "That was a rhetorical question and doesn't count against one of my three."

Harriet gave a bemused smirk.

"It sounds like you don't have anything to investigate," Devlin suggested.

Autumn whirled on him. "Except that whatever Bernard was up to got him killed. Nobody in this fiasco is innocent."

Devlin clenched his fists. "Except sometimes you find yourself in the middle of a homicide that has nothing to do with you or face-to-face with a criminal, and the only way out is to leave behind everyone and everything you've ever known." He went nose-to-nose with Autumn as his chest heaved with boiling frustration.

"Bernard isn't innocent," Joy murmured.

Autumn didn't move away from Devlin, only looked up at him with an expression of compassion and understanding. She apparently understood Devlin wasn't referring to Bernard.

What had come over him?

He'd made a good life for Kimmy and himself—a new beginning where Kimmy knew nothing of her mother's past and deceitfulness. And he wasn't prepared to make another start in another town, to leave Kimmy wondering what had forced them to keep moving away from friends and familiarity until she grew old enough to understand

and to hate her father for the life into which she'd been boxed.

Autumn placed her hands on his arms. "Devlin, I was referring to Bernard. It wasn't my intention to upset you."

He tried to relax his fists, feeling the small crescent indentations his fingernails had left in his palms. He regained his composure. Joy watched with interest, and Harriet arched a bushy eyebrow.

"Good for you," Joy drawled. "Man's gotta right to pitch a fit now and again."

Devlin kept his gaze on Autumn. Pitch a fit? How did one pitch a fit? Was that some type of curveball?

Autumn's hands on his arms grounded him. He took a steadying breath. "I shouldn't have. I'm sorry." As he started to step back from Autumn, she squeezed him gently, keeping him fixed in front of her.

"I think you've earned the right to be upset, considering your situation."

They stood close enough that he could see sunlight reflecting off her small diamond-studded earrings. He envisioned reaching forward and tucking one of her dark, silky curls behind her ear, but he wouldn't cross that boundary. He didn't have express permission to cross it.

He licked his lips and retreated a step. "I'm fine." He was definitely *not* fine. "You have other questions?"

Autumn lowered her hands to her sides. Was there reluctance on her part to move away? Devlin dismissed the thought.

"Does Joy have any idea where the art is stored? Where Bernard transported it to?"

Devlin smiled, appreciating Autumn's acknowledgement of Joy's contribution, even though she was skeptical of Devlin's psychic abilities.

Autumn gave him the barest eye roll and a small grin.

Joy, interrupting the sparks Devlin felt between him and Autumn, recited an address.

Devlin extended a hand toward Autumn.

Autumn's breath caught in her throat, and she instinctively reached out.

Before she finished her motion to take his hand, he said, "Give me your phone. I'll type in the address."

"Right." She cleared her throat.

She pulled her phone out of her pocket and handed it to him. Devlin entered the address into Autumn's maps app and handed it back to her. The barest brushing of fingers sent his heart skipping.

"You get one more question," Harriet said.

"I'll save it for later."

"You sure you don't want him to use the crystal ball? You're missing out," the marshal insisted.

"No, thank you," Autumn replied.

Devlin didn't want to show Autumn the crystal ball. When a ghost centered itself in the crystal, an onlooker could see wisps of the apparition or scenes, usually enough to identify persons or objects, but the clarity wasn't spectacular. It gave only visual stimulus and no sound. The crystal ball provided help as a performance tool to create belief in the skeptic or warm the heart of someone suffering, but it wasn't helpful for the nuts and bolts of getting information where words performed better.

"Alrighty. Let's load up," Harriet said. "I'll take over

protection duty, so I'll drive Devlin and Kimmy to the police station. Special Agent Bentley, you are free to pursue your forged art."

Autumn glanced at Harriet's Ford. "Your truck doesn't have space for a child car seat. Why don't I drive Devlin and Kimmy? We'll follow you to the station, and I'll turn them over to you there."

Devlin stared at Autumn, trying to read her expression. Was she fulfilling a law enforcement duty? Was she securing more time with him so she could ask more questions? Or was there something in their chemistry together that had her wanting to linger?

Foolish notion.

Joy placed the back of her hand on her forehead. "What do I do? I am adrift. I'm Spanish moss, limp and stagnant on a mighty oak."

Devlin took a few steps away from Autumn and Harriet to speak with Joy, whose dramatic flair threatened to make Devlin give an ill-timed laugh. "Why don't you stick around? If you think of anything that might be helpful to Agent Bentley, let me know and I'll relay it to her. I appreciate all of your help so far. I'm sorry you lost Bernard. We can hold a candlelight service for him tonight."

He wondered what kept Joy anchored in this world. He'd assumed it had been Bernard, yet now that he'd departed, she still hadn't moved on. But helping Joy cross to the spirit would have to wait until he and Kimmy were safe. In the meantime, if Joy had anything helpful to offer Special Agent Bentley, Devlin could pass it along to her.

. . .

TEN MINUTES LATER, Autumn was driving her car with a groggy Kimmy sitting in the back seat. The ruffled girl wore a scowl at having been awakened from her nap.

Autumn itched to ask Devlin more questions about the dubious forged art in order to brainstorm about what Bernard had been truly up to, but she couldn't discuss the topic of violence, fraud, and murder in front of Kimmy. If Autumn was being honest, she felt equally curious about Oscar. Was this man the reason Devlin was confined to witness protection?

So many burning questions, but the only time she had left with him was this silent car ride to the police station. Beside her, Devlin flipped a tarot card between his fingers with dizzying dexterity. Unable to give him words of comfort, she contemplated holding his hand, but the gesture would be absurd. She barely knew him.

Maybe Devlin could somehow keep his identity. Did one homicide doom him to starting over?

She glanced back at Kimmy. "You said she's in first grade?"

"That's right." He smiled. "She's so smart. Loves to read. We're on *The Magic Tree House* series. Do you have any children?"

"No." She and her ex-fiancé had discussed having children but usually under the context that offspring would curb his career path, and neither of them knew how to fit them into a life where they traveled so much with their investigations. "I'm not in a relationship. I haven't been for quite some time. I was engaged, but as you are already aware, it didn't work out."

"Right."

"Relationships don't tend to work out when one person doesn't value monogamy."

"Very true."

Devlin's bleary tone had Autumn wondering if he too had experience with infidelity in a prior relationship.

She decided to steer the conversation elsewhere. "Does your daughter know about the g-h-o—"

"Don't spell it. Her vocabulary is expanding like the Big Bang. She doesn't know I'm a medium."

"How long have you had that ability?"

Devlin glanced at her, probably wondering if she was teasing. But she wasn't. She might not admit to believing in ghosts, but the longer she spent around Devlin, the less his abilities seemed like a performance. Autumn didn't have a rational explanation for his behavior, but he seemed like a decent person and she didn't encounter many of those in the art forgery world.

"Since I was sixteen."

"Sixteenth birthday?"

"No. It happened after an accident, actually. I was in Tahoe skiing with my family and took a fall. After the concussion—*viola*—I began seeing apparitions. My mom had the gift, though I hadn't known about it until I thought I was going crazy and she intervened."

"Do you think," Autumn's eyes darted to Kimmy and back to Devlin, "she'll have the ability?"

"I guess I'd better keep her safe from head injuries so we don't have to find out."

"Your skills seem to serve you well. You wouldn't wish that on someone else?"

"No. Not the judgment that goes with it. I kept it a

secret in my previous... before," he kept himself from saying too much in front of Kimmy. "I'm exploiting it in this life with the justification that I'm helping people. Maybe not like I used to, but I'm helping."

"Used to? Oh. You said you were a paramedic, right?" Autumn probed.

"Yeah. *Was.*"

Silence rode with them for a moment as Autumn tried to choose her words and questions carefully. "What do you mean by judgment?"

Devlin shot her an incredulous look. "The judgment that I'm a charlatan. That this is all a show. The judgment you yourself passed on me. I can't even tell if you're asking these questions because you're genuinely interested or because you're patronizing me."

Autumn laid her hand on his, keeping one on the steering wheel. "I am genuinely interested, Devlin. I'm not saying I'm a believer, but I promise to reserve judgment from here on out." She pulled her hand back and rested it on her thigh.

The warmth of his skin lingered on her hand. It conjured images of their bodies close in the bathroom and his gentle touch as he'd bandaged her arm.

"Well, you have your address. So after the police station, you can find your stash and chalk this up to a strange encounter of the third kind."

She suspected Devlin was attempting to make a joke, but his words contained more sadness than jubilance.

"And what will you do?" she asked.

"Collect the pieces. Start over." He breathed as if a heavy weight settled on his chest. "Any career suggestions not related to medicine or the super-natural?"

"You have to start over as long as Oscar's still out there?"

"Yes."

"Daddy, I'm hungry."

"Okay, Kimmy. We'll get you another snack at the police station."

"Why are we going to the police?"

"Aunt Harriet wants to see some of her friends."

"Are you police?" Kimmy asked Autumn.

"I'm FBI. We stop bad people, too."

WHEN THEY ARRIVED at the police station, Autumn took the flank with Harriet leading the way and Devlin and Kimmy wedged between them.

The police station presented a delay Autumn didn't need, but she wouldn't take the homicide lightly. Obviously, a murder investigation took precedence over finding forged art. Except that nothing could be done for Bernard, whereas the art could be secretly moved while she was detained at the station. Local PD could make this meeting swift and mutually respect a fellow law enforcement officer, or they could be upset Autumn had left the scene and detain her just to prove a point.

As Harriet spoke to the assistant at the counter, Autumn looked down at Kimmy, who stared at the high counter and faded sea-green walls, before her small green eyes saw the bowl of Halloween candy on the counter. When Autumn winked at her, Kimmy smiled.

In a few minutes, Devlin and Kimmy were being whisked away toward the back of the police station.

Just like that, they disappeared. Autumn didn't get to say goodbye. She'd never thanked Devlin for the information—though she had yet to validate it. Once she had, it wasn't as though she'd be able to look him up on the internet and call him. Harriet would be working on a new identity as soon as the police interview had concluded.

Well, goodbyes were less important perhaps when she'd only known him a few short hours. And, given the chance to say goodbye, what would she have said? "Can I buy you a drink sometime?" To which he would reply, "Sure, Special Agent Bentley, look me up in WITSEC."

It was better this way. Nothing awkward.

He disappears with his adorable daughter down a corridor and doesn't look back.

Except, she realized, Devlin had looked back—one wide-eyed glance so brief she didn't even have time to respond.

"You're Special Agent Autumn Bentley of the FBI?"

Autumn turned to see a balding man, tall enough he probably played competitive basketball before age and a protuberant waist slowed him down.

Autumn held up her credentials. "I am."

"I'd like to ask you a few questions about the shooting."

CHAPTER 6

Oscar Mooney watched the five o'clock news from his small, lumpy sofa. Television and internet provided his only link to the US. In fact, they had been his only link for six years. Six years in exile.

He'd been moving around Mexico, leapfrogging from one dump to the next. This last year he'd spent renting an apartment on the third floor of a brothel. A brothel!

Prior to this, he'd been thriving in bustling Chicago in a penthouse with a spectacular view of Lake Michigan. Now, avoiding the law and living on a tight budget, he languished in a miserable third-world existence. He'd taken his riches with him—the liquid assets which hadn't been frozen when he'd accidentally shot Rachael—but he couldn't spend money and attract attention to himself.

Rachael's husband was probably basking in his successful escape. At least he too had to live in obscurity... hiding in witness protection.

Because the Gambino crime family was providing protection for him while he lived in Mexico, Oscar would follow their careful instructions delivered through Smith, his only contact to the life he once had.

When the television image changed to a video feed taken on a mobile phone, Oscar dropped the can of cerveza he was holding. He scrambled for the remote and turned up the volume to hear the newscaster.

"Earlier today in Sacramento, a man was shot and killed at a psychic reading establishment. A bystander took video on his phone of two suspects fleeing the scene of the crime. Authorities have yet to make an arrest for the murder of..."

Oscar snatched his phone off the charger and called his contact. "Smith, it's Oscar. I found Rachael's husband."

"What do you mean?"

"I'm staring at him on the five o'clock news." On screen, the video played again—Aaron, his beard reduced to a little facial hair, climbed into a car with a woman in a navy suit. Businesswoman or law enforcement? Had he remarried?

"Where is he?" Smith demanded.

"Sacramento. At least he was at the time of the video. He was running away from the scene of a crime."

"What crime?"

"A murder."

Had Racheal's husband murdered someone? Surely he wasn't capable of killing anyone. If so, he'd fallen a long way from the Boy Scout he'd once been.

"Okay. Okay. This is good. I've got contacts in Sacramento. We can get to him when they arrest him."

"Get to him?" Oscar asked.

"If he's dead, he can't testify and the entire case against you falls apart, right?"

He'd imagined the death of Racheal's husband—Aaron's—a thousand times and even envisioned his own hands encircling the man's throat. He was the reason Racheal had died. And Smith had both the resources and resolve to actually kill Aaron.

"Oscar? Are you listening to me? This is your ticket to freedom, right?"

Oscar cleared his throat. "Right. Of course. But shouldn't we make sure he's the only source? We need to know if he or Rachael created files or made a video."

Oscar wanted to be there when Aaron took a bullet—like his wife had. So he invented a reason to stall Aaron's death, giving himself time to cross the border and reach Sacramento. Oscar'd had a few fake IDs created over the years. Maybe he'd risk flying.

Smith released a low whistle. "Okay. You want him tortured. You're cold-blooded, but I like it. I'll let you know when we snatch him."

The phone call disconnected.

Tortured?

Oscar watched the video replay of the news report.

He'd always considered her death a waste. Rachael had married some rough-around-the-edges paramedic with a conscience, and he had gotten her killed.

Rachael. Oscar thought of the beautiful, long-legged junior lawyer at his law firm. Her lovely blonde hair had been thick as honey. He recalled the feel of his fingertips sinking into the soft flesh of her hips and the sound of her sweet voice whispering his name.

He clenched his fists. But then she'd shattered everything he'd spent a decade building by choosing Aaron over him. As a result, Oscar had languished for the last six years, moving from one hellhole to the next.

Not anymore.

He'd found Rachael's husband, and he would exact his revenge.

Devlin waited in the room alone. Harriet had taken Kimmy to get snacks at one point, after which Devlin answered the police questions about events at his rental building. They seemed frustrated that he didn't know more. He didn't divulge the warehouse information he'd given Autumn, though he did mention Autumn thought Bernard was somehow involved in moving fraudulent art.

Devlin was then forced to explain why he'd fled the scene of the crime. His reasoning was because, before or after the police had arrived, news reporters would have followed. Devlin's face on news footage could be one of many ways Oscar might find him.

Devlin answered no police questions about the reason he dwelled in witness protection or who might be after him. If the police department wanted that information, they could contact the US Marshals' office, which could decide if they would divulge the backstory.

In the end, the questioning officers seemed annoyed at

the lack of knowledge about the circumstances surrounding Bernard's death, and they cast disparaging looks whenever they tried to clarify exactly what the psychic Devlin had done. He offered to show them his crystal ball, but they declined, which was a good thing, because he realized it wasn't in his briefcase.

Alone in the interrogation room, Devlin wondered if the waiting was part of the process or if the officers had left to get themselves a Frappuccino. At least he knew Kimmy was in good hands. Harriet was like an aunt to her. Aside from sweet-talking Harriet into giving her Halloween candy, Kimmy would stay safe.

Joy appeared and began rambling in a high-pitched quake. "Oh, calamity." She fanned herself. "I'm hotter than a sinner in church. The creek's a risin' and your girl-friend's riding toward trouble. All this stress is gonna make me lose my religion."

"Joy, slow down. Tell me slowly. But first, are the room's recording devices on?"

"No."

"Okay. What has you so worked up?"

"FBI Special Agent Autumn Bentley is on her way to the abandoned building."

"Right. I gave her the address so she can go collect the art."

"It isn't art."

"I thought we established it's printed, fabricated replicas?"

"Yes. But the printed, pasted replicas aren't what's important. What's important is the canvas."

"The canvas?"

Joy nodded exuberanantly. "It's not normal canvas. The canvas is made of compressed heroin."

"Compressed heroin!" Heroin that had crossed the border looking like expensive works of art—to the untrained eye, no doubt.

"How do they compress it?" he asked.

Joy gaped at him. "Do I look like a heroin dealer?"

"So, Autumn is on her way to uncover a drug-smuggling operation, not art forgery." The situation sounded far too dangerous for a one-agent operation. "Is that why Bernard was shot?"

"Rival gang."

"But why shoot the delivery man? Unless… unless they already know where the shipment is."

"They already know," Joy said dismally.

"Autumn's going to find an empty loft or walk into an ambush of armed drug dealers?"

"I don't know, but I'm afraid it might be the latter."

Devlin pinched the bridge of his nose. He wished ghosts would be more forthcoming with information, but sometimes it felt like he had to ask the right question. "I need to warn Autumn." As he stood, he felt a sinking sensation. "I don't know her number. But she called Harriet." He brightened. "She'll have Autumn's number on her incoming call list. I need to warn the FBI agent."

The door to his interview room opened, and a uniformed police officer entered. He wasn't one of the ones who'd interviewed him, and Devlin hadn't met him yet.

"Officer, I needed to speak with US Marshal Harriet Williams."

"Yes, sir. I can get a message to him for you." He motioned for Devlin to follow him out of the room and down the hall.

"It's a she. And I need to tell her Special Agent Bently could be walking into a dangerous situation."

The officer glanced from side to side through the station as they walked. "I'll let her know." His posture looked stiff and his attention focused.

Odd. Devlin had been under Autumn's scrutiny for the last few hours, so he'd been expecting a litany of questions. Who's Bently? What is the dangerous situation? Why does he care about it?

Instead, he escorted Devlin with detached professionalism. When they exited the building, Devlin blinked under the late afternoon light.

They reached an unmarked police car away from the station, and the hair on Devlin's neck stood on end.

"Wait. Where are we going?"

The officer opened the trunk of the car. Searing pain coursed through Devlin's body as he went rigid and fell forward.

Everything went black.

AUTUMN SAT in a cafe eating a Reuben sandwich. She hadn't eaten all day and wasn't sure how long investigating the stolen art at the abandoned building would take, so she stopped for a bite to eat.

She sipped a pumpkin latte, which seemed appropriate since it was Halloween. Maybe she'd splurge and get one of those pumpkin-shaped cookies in the display window.

As she ate, she thought about the only other time she'd fired her weapon. Like her current case, it had begun with hunting forged art and ended with a twist.

Autumn had thrown herself into her work after discovering her fiancé's infidelity. Because he was also an FBI agent, as was the other woman, she'd wanted to avoid the awkward looks from her colleagues—some mixture of disdain and pity, which Autumn couldn't stomach. She'd focused on her assigned case, determined to force her pain and mortification into submission with eighty-hour work weeks.

Someone had been making forgeries of Ming Dynasty china. Autumn followed the trail to intercept a shipment at the docks in San Francisco, but her snitch had told her the wrong pier number.

So instead of tracking David Ying's shipment of fake Ming Dynasty art, Autumn had found herself in front of Karl Ying's shipment of trafficked women. She'd discovered she was ill-prepared for a situation of this magnitude, so she had taken clandestine photos and called in the illegal activity to the FBI office. But she worried that by the time the FBI assembled a team, the women would be gone.

She also wasn't Jane Bond with a few spare tracking devices to tag the moving vans. And with more than one truck, she had no way of following them all.

As Autumn had watched, she'd noticed a man who seemed to be the leader among them. As the vans loaded and left one by one, Autumn stayed and kept Ying's man in sight. She'd hoped to capture him and give her FBI colleagues the means to discover the whereabouts of the other women. When the last group of a dozen women were being loaded onto a van, a woman decided to rebel. She screamed and attacked one of the armed men. The leader backhanded her, knocking her to the ground. A young girl of about twelve years of age had used the distraction to bolt to her freedom.

The aggressor, three times her size and with longer legs, had sprinted after her. There'd been no way she could outrun him. Three of Ying's other men had kept the rest of the women tightly together.

Autumn had come out of hiding, gun raised. "FBI! Freeze!"

With murderous intent in his eyes, the running man hadn't slowed. He could crush the small girl to death if he tackled her on the hard concrete pier. Autumn fired one shot into his leg, and the man toppled to the ground.

The rest of Ying's men, probably assuming the FBI agent wasn't foolish enough to be on the pier at night alone, fled.

The man, injured and bleeding on the ground, pulled his gun and fired wildly in the direction of Autumn and the girl, now crouched behind crates. The bullets landed harmlessly in the surrounding cargo crates as he expended all of his rounds. Then, Autumn had restrained him.

In a bizarre mix-up, Autumn had saved one little girl and freed a dozen women. Her superior, angry that Autumn had put herself in danger, had reluctantly admitted the traffic ring had been exposed and taken down because of Autumn.

The press would later morph the story into one where a heroic lone FBI agent faced down six armed men in a dangerous hostage stand-off and single-handedly disarmed a deadly situation under threat to her own life.

Ironically, her career-making case was related to human trafficking and not even her trained specialty of forged art. But the headlines had done nothing to soothe her heartbreak. She'd merely been working overtime, and that hardly felt like heroism.

DEVLIN WOKE to darkness and a hard, bumping surface. He tried to roll but banged his knees on a low ceiling. He groaned. Had he been out for minutes or hours? Probably minutes. The body could quickly recover consciousness after a stun gun.

Please, please let Kimmy still be safe with Harriet. Devlin felt around the cramped trunk of the car he'd been crammed inside, realizing his hands were cuffed together in front of him. His fingers identified the borders of his prison and the coarse fiber carpeting along the floor and edges. Finding the rear of the trunk, he peeled back the lining and felt the hard plastic beneath. Continuing his efforts, he searched for the cord—the piece he could tug to release the trunk.

Hope leaped in his chest when he found the stiff line. Caution stopped him. What would happen when he pulled it? If he was being driven down a road with traffic, he'd be seen, and someone would call the police. If he was somewhere remote, he'd be giving himself away.

"Joy?"

"You've got yourself in a pickle. Mama always said that. I suppose I never stopped to think what that means. In a pickle. I always liked pickles." She wasn't visible, but her chatter brought a certain sense of relief.

"Joy, are there any other cars around?" he asked.

"Hold your horses. I'm checking. Uh, no. We're on Highway 99."

"Heading which way?"

"South."

Where could the rogue cop be taking him? Icy chills coursed down Devlin's spine. A crooked cop meant Oscar was involved. No doubt there. And of course, the Gambino family.

Unless someone thought Bernard had shared valuable information with him. Then Mexican drug dealers were involved. Devlin wasn't sure which was worse, or which would have him joining Bernard in the next life.

"Is Kimmy safe?"

"Hang on," Joy replied.

Devlin waited in the dark, feeling the seconds tick by like hours. He imagined Kimmy's life without him. Harriet would protect her. But would she adopt her? No. Did that mean foster care was in her future?

"She's happy as a lark hanging out with Harriet. Safe."

Devlin breathed a sigh of relief. *"Crystal balls and crow calls."*

"What does that mean?" Joy asked.

"Something my mother used to say. It's something you

might say when you feel fortunate, like 'thank heavens' or 'my lucky stars.'"

"What's it mean?"

"Well, crystal balls are a link to the spiritual world, and it's fortuitous to have one. And when a crow calls, your fortune is about to change so you're supposed to listen carefully."

Joy sighed. "Well, slap my head and call me silly! That's entirely too complicated. Just say 'thank heavens.'"

Devlin grunted. *So says the ghost who usually uses ten words when two would suffice.*

"My saying is richer," he replied. "And with a more profound meaning."

"Are all psychics so profound?"

"My mother was."

"What happened to her?"

"She died when I was twenty-five."

"How awful, dear. That sticks in your throat like a hair in your jam. Both of you so young."

"She had me when she was forty, after she thought she'd never be able to bear a child. She always called me her gift. Her only regret in life was ever picking up that first cigarette."

Joy fell silent before clearing her throat. "Well, regarding your present dilemma. I'm as nervous as a long-tailed cat in a room full of rocking chairs. Does your crystal ball tell us how to get you out of this trunk?"

Devlin snorted. He didn't have anything—no briefcase, no phone, and no crystal ball. His briefcase and phone were probably with his captor. His crystal ball was...

"Joy! My crystal ball is still in Autumn's car. It rolled

out of my briefcase. It must have rolled under the seat, because it wasn't in sight as I collected the scattered contents of my briefcase when we arrived at the police station."

"What good does it do you under the seat of her car?"

"You can reach it."

"And do what?"

"Get her attention." He tried to temper the irritation in his voice from the anxiety over the time-sensitive nature of his sudden plan.

"How?" Joy asked.

"Do you remember the time we showed Bernard your face in the crystal ball?"

"I remember. It was a bonny spring day, raining cats and dogs—"

"Then you changed the view to the picture of a beach to remind him of your honeymoon. Maybe you can do that with Autumn—show her images." Crystal balls didn't generate sound, so she'd have to use visuals to communicate with Autumn.

"I can do that! I can do that!" Joy's exuberant tone filled Devlin with hope.

The car fell silent except for the hum of tires on the road. Now, Devlin had to wait—his future was in the hands of a ghost in mourning and an FBI agent who'd been glad to be rid of him only a few hours ago.

CHAPTER 7

*A*utumn drove with purpose, following the GPS route to the abandoned psychiatric hospital where she'd supposedly find forged art. Art forged under the Mexican cartel dealer Cesar Torres. She'd called her FBI colleague to get a short biography about the man who turned out to be notorious for smuggling heroin into the US. His route extended along the West Coast from Tijuana to Portland, the I-5 corridor.

So why switch to fabricated art—and the sort of art that wouldn't hold up to scrutiny?

Meanwhile, her information had originated from a medium with a checkered past. Well, if Devlin had been lying to her, she'd know soon enough, and she knew where to find him. If Devlin left the police station, Autumn still had Harriet's number on her phone.

Autumn felt inclined to believe Devlin, though, for the life of her, she couldn't figure out why. Instinct, she supposed. She knew how to spot fakes and frauds, and the more time she spent with Devlin, the more he seemed authentic.

A flash of light caught her attention. Looking toward the passenger side, a glow emitted from under the seat. She remembered Devlin's briefcase had spilled in her back seat. Had he left a flashlight behind in her car? His phone?

She pulled over at the next gas station and parked the car. After walking around to the passenger side, she bent down to dig under the seat. Her hands touched something smooth—a card. She closed her index finger and middle finger over it and pulled it out. One side had orange paisley decorations mixed with burgundy and blue. The other side had a dancing skeleton under a full moon. 'Death' was scrawled on the bottom.

Ugh. She didn't need to see Devlin's creepy tarot card on Halloween while driving to an abandoned nuthouse.

The flashing light continued to shine blue from under the seat. Autumn reached in again, and this time she felt a cold, smooth orb, larger than a billiard ball. She pulled it to her and stood.

Devlin's crystal ball.

She didn't remember having seen it glow in DEVLIN'S PSYCHIC READINGS consultation room. She inspected it for some type of switch but found none. Running her hands over the surface, she thought perhaps it was heat or motion activated, but the glow didn't change under her touch. Autumn stared more deeply into the orb. Did she see Devlin?

Was she hallucinating?

Dark hair and a firm jaw. Green eyes.

The image appeared blurred, and Autumn blinked to clear her vision, which didn't help. A glass-bottle haze stood between her and a clear view of Devlin, but the man was unmistakably him.

The picture zoomed out from his face. He was walking with a police escort out of the police station. Although no sound emitted from the orb, Autumn could tell they weren't speaking. The cop led Devlin to a vehicle—alone and away from the station. Autumn's gut clenched with an ominous feeling.

Was this something about to happen, happening at this moment, or that had already happened?

The police officer opened his trunk and, in one swift motion, positioned himself behind Devlin. Devlin went stiff before collapsing forward, and his assailant folded his body into the trunk. The entire event happened in a mere thirty seconds.

Devlin!

Autumn pulled out her phone and called US Marshal Williams.

"Agent Bentley. I'm surprised to hear back from you so soon. Did you want that third question?"

"Do you have visual on Devlin?"

"What? No. He's in the police station surrounded by a dozen cops."

"Is Kimmy with you?"

"Yes. What's going on?"

"You wouldn't believe me if I told you. Or maybe you would, because I'm staring at Devlin's crystal ball right now. Can you get eyes on Devlin and confirm he's safe? Keep Kimmy with you."

"I don't like your tone, agent."

Even as Harriet complained, Autumn could hear the shuffling of movements and steps. Harriet asked to see Devlin.

More footsteps.

A door opening.

Voices rushed and worried.

"I'll call you back."

"Harriet—"

But Harriet disconnected the call.

Autumn swore and kicked the tire of her car. She slammed the passenger door shut before getting back in the driver's seat. She looked down at Devlin's crystal ball still in her hand. The light and the image had extinguished.

Autumn stared out of the windshield. She could continue on to her destination and let the US Marshal find Devlin. After all, the alarm had been raised. Not Autumn's problem anymore. But Autumn had the power to find him in the palm of her hand... literally.

"Devlin?" Autumn said to the orb.

It remained dormant. Autumn thought about what Devlin had said about the crystal ball—it was some type of gateway to spirits.

"Joy?"

The orb pulsed with low azure light. She glanced around her. Was she honestly going to address a ghost? Strange things and her pride aside, Devlin was in danger.

"Joy, who took Devlin? Was it Oscar's men or Cesar Torres's men?"

An inky black question mark rippled through the ball as if in water.

"Where is Devlin now?"

A picture of a sign appeared: Highway 99 South. The image was followed by a mile-marker sign.

"Thanks, Joy." Autumn set the orb down in the passenger seat, started her engine, and drove toward Devlin.

ALONE IN THE DARK, Devlin's thoughts spiraled into terrifying places. He'd always believed Oscar blamed him for Rachael's death, even though Oscar had been the one to involve Rachael in the Gambino crime family's deviousness. He suspected Oscar wanted to kill him.

In fact, when he'd first seen the gunman kick open his door earlier today, he had thought the hitman had come for him—that Oscar had found him. Oh, the relief he'd felt when it became apparent Bernard had been the target. He'd felt guilty for that relief—being alive at Bernard's expense.

But now, he'd been found, anyway. Except, the cop hadn't had him killed immediately. Perhaps he was willing to get paid for kidnapping and not murder—all the while transporting him to the real killer. Or perhaps he wanted the body to be deposited somewhere remote.

"Devlin."

"Joy, I'm so glad to hear your voice."

"Special Agent Bentley's on her way."

"Really?" Devlin felt surprised by the thrill and hope Joy's simple sentence gave him. "Just like that?"

"I showed her your abduction. She called the US Marshal, who confirmed you were missing. Then, she turned her car around."

"Thank you. Thank you."

"She a fine little specimen of a woman. I bet she's as cute as a pearl button when she wears a summer dress."

"Who?"

"Who? I may be dead, but I'm not blind. You think Special Agent Bentley is attractive, and it shows in your body language."

"You and I are not on the sort of personal level to have this conversation." He kept his tone chidingly playful, but the thought of discussing his feelings with a ghost made him squirm.

He hadn't spoken to anyone about women or relationships since before entering WITSEC, except for Harriet stating the program didn't require celibacy. Yet, careless interactions and divulging his identity would risk his life and Kimmy's.

"When it comes to women, you're a boat without an oar. Have you got something better to do than discuss women while in the trunk of a car as you're driven to your death?"

Devlin sighed. "Sure. Why don't I romanticize a relationship where Autumn rescues me and I kiss her senseless, prompting her to sacrifice an FBI career to join me in a dull life in WITSEC."

"Or you could think more on the short-term rather than the improbable."

"What's that mean?"

Joy snorted. "Aren't you precious? I'm referring to a one-night stand."

"I'm not setting that sort of example for my daughter."

"Honey, she doesn't have to know."

"I'd know."

Joy sighed. "Suit yourself. I'm going back to watch the determined FBI heroine ride to your rescue... I guarantee she's thinking about at least a one-night stand."

"Really?"

No reply came.

Autumn knew his secret, which meant she was already a woman Devlin didn't have to lie to. Still, he couldn't embark on a relationship under these circumstances.

Besides, he needed to focus on the escape plan. The rogue cop would know his career was shattered the minute Autumn caught up to him. Jail would probably be as horrible a prospect for an officer as failing the Gambino family would be.

Cornered animals became wild and unpredictable.

THE CAR SLOWED, and Devlin worried that was a bad sign. "Joy, where are we?"

"Oh my lands, honey. We are nowhere. The side of a deserted road off Highway 99."

"That sounds ominous." Was this his place of execution? "How far away is Autumn?"

Joy didn't reply.

"Joy?"

"Hold your britches. I'm checking." Her tone turned doleful. "She's too far, honey. Too far."

Since rescue wasn't an option, Devlin contemplated the other means of escape he'd been conjuring while riding in the trunk.

When the trunk opened, searing light blinded him. Devlin lashed out a leg, feeling it land in the soft flesh of the cop's abdomen.

The cop let out a cough as Devlin leapt out of the trunk. He plowed into the cop, who was hunched over from the kick. But the cop grabbed him around the waist and hurled Devlin aside.

With his hands cuffed, Devlin couldn't catch himself. He tried, stumbled, and landed on his back. A boot drove into his stomach. Devlin gasped at the pain before curling into a ball and taking the next kick to his guarded side.

"Get up," the cop snarled.

Blinking, Devlin looked up at the cop. Was he a real policeman? Oath to protect and serve? His crew cut looked the part, and no one at the station had given him a second glance when he'd escorted Devlin outside. His badge read MAZZONE.

Devlin uncoiled and struggled to his feet. "If you let me go, I'll tell you the location of heroin. Lots of heroin." Devlin glanced at Joy who appeared to be biting her nails.

Mazzone grinned, revealing a mouth of metal—gold teeth and silver caps in a haphazard arrangement.

Devlin cringed.

"And how does mister do-gooder, fake fortune-teller know about heroin?" He paused a beat and then added, "Let's make a different bargain."

Mazzone's low, menacing voice made Devlin realize he'd played the wrong hand or maybe no right hand existed with a man like this. Visions of the Tower tarot card flashed before him—a high, straight spire on a mountaintop, being struck by lightning and set ablaze. Upright, it symbolized upheaval and disaster.

Devlin squeezed his eyes shut and pressed his hands to his aching abdomen.

"How about you tell me about this intriguing stash of heroin, and I don't mention Oscar's daughter to him?"

Devlin's lids flew open.

"Ha. He doesn't know, does he?" Mazzone smirked. "Yeah. I heard the story about your wife. The timing is right."

Devlin shook his head as his temple throbbed as if a vice squeezed around his head.

Mazzone ran a lazy tongue across his teeth. "Tell you what. You cooperate—every step of the way—and I'll neglect to mention the kid."

With a dry swallow, Devlin nodded.

"Now, tell me about this stash."

AFTER THEIR CONVERSATION and a bathroom break behind bushes, Devlin was crammed back into the trunk of the cop's car. He had no way of knowing if Mazzone would betray him and tell Oscar about Kimmy even though Devlin had given the location of the heroin.

With a click, the trunk closed, and Devlin found himself once again plunged into darkness. As uncomfortable as lying in the trunk was, it afforded him the opportunity to scheme with Joy—something he wouldn't have been able to do if he sat in Mazzone's back seat.

"Joy?"

"I'm right here, sweetie."

"I'm sorry about Bernard." It occurred to Devlin that even though he'd been a paramedic, Bernard was only the second person he'd seen shot directly in front of him.

At the time, he'd flashed back to that terrible day when Rachael had been shot, but his medical training had enabled him to compartmentalize the violence so he could treat Bernard—like it had when Rachael had been shot.

To a sweet Southern delicacy like Joy, watching Bernard get shot must've been deeply traumatizing.

"I'd hoped he had longer to live… long enough for atonement. Long enough for the Holy Spirit to lay his hands upon Bernard's bosom and turn his wayward ways into days of repentance." She continued, but Devlin tuned her out to avoid thinking of Bernard's bosom.

Joy droned on about Bernard's salvation, and yet her spirit lingered here, while Bernard had moved on. Perhaps he had been more at peace with his life of crime than she was with her life as Mrs. Porter.

Joy sniffed. "But enough about me, hon. We need to get your life in order."

"Can you check on Special Agent Bentley? Maybe give her an update on my location?"

"Sure, pumpkin. I'll be back faster than a hot knife through butter. You know she thinks you're easy on the eyes. Like apple pie with a dollop of vanilla ice cream."

"Thanks." Devlin hadn't heard that Southern analogy before, and he felt at a loss for the appropriate response.

"Did you know Autumn visited her grandmother weekly in her nursing home before she died?"

"I do now."

"That was back when she went to college. As an FBI agent, though, she's somewhat of a hero. Solved this Ying case and saved a girl's life. All in a day's work with a woman like that. Oh, and she cooks. I hear she makes Sunday morning biscuits so fluffy and delicious they'd make you slap your mama."

Devlin pinched the bridge of his nose. Was Joy honestly trying to match them together? A matchmaking ghost—this was a first for him.

"Joy," he began, hoping to pull her back to reality, "for heaven's sakes, I'm captive in the trunk of a dirty cop's car. I'm not interested in Autumn romantically, and I'm not discussing her biscuits."

"Why? Are you gluten-free?" She cackled. "Although, when you put it that way, it does conjure a different image. Besides, it's not like you have something better to do... " Her voice trailed off as her presence dissipated.

Devlin suppressed a sigh. Joy was helping tremendously. Perhaps Devlin could have indulged the ghost. He couldn't recall the last time he'd gossiped with another person about an eligible woman ... or her biscuits.

Joy'd been correct—Devlin had nothing better to do while scrunched up in the back of a trunk. Why not fantasize about a beautiful woman with a self-assured style? He could forget the endless hum of the tires and the hard surface by envisioning running a finger along Autumn's soft skin. Her lips would curl in an invitation, and then she'd stretch up to her toes and press her lips to his.

Better than apple pie.

Yeah, right.

He had nothing to offer a remarkable woman like that. He was a former paramedic turned pseudo-psychic reader who'd become a widower and father all in one horrible and miraculous night.

He needed Autumn to be a decent law enforcement officer who helped him out of a sense of duty before bidding him good day.

Bidding him good day?

What was she? Annie Oakley? Joy's Southern references were melting his brain. Next, he'd be imagining Autumn tipping her hat before riding into the sunset.

Autumn in tight jeans and a cowgirl hat. Dang. Yup, she was apple pie with a side of vanilla ice cream.

Devlin rolled his shoulders and adjusted his position in the tight space.

Save yourself, Devlin. Figure out a plan.

He'd escaped Oscar once—he could do it again.

CHAPTER 8

Oscar exited the plane at the San Jose airport. His fake passport, which had cost a small fortune when he'd bought it a few years ago, enabled him to cross the border, through the San Diego airport, and up to San Jose. After six years of a stagnant life, suddenly everything was moving fast.

Smith had called him before he'd boarded the plane to tell him some cop in his pocket would be snatching Aaron soon, and, oh by the way, congratulations, you're a father. Oscar had assumed the baby had died when he'd shot Racheal.

Oscar stopped at the restroom, relieved himself, and then stared into the mirror. Who was this man staring back at him? He wasn't some treacherous villain for the Gambino family. He'd been a respected lawyer. The mob had taken that from him just as Aaron had taken Racheal... and apparently his child.

Splashing water on his face revived him. He honestly didn't know what he planned to do when he saw Aaron.

He'd loved Rachael—even though she'd been married to Aaron. If Oscar wanted to reinstate himself in full capacity with the Gambino family as a lawyer in Chicago, he had to eliminate the one person standing between himself and his freedom—Aaron.

After exiting the restroom, he strolled out of the airport while checking his text messages. It was eight in the evening, and Smith's dirty cop had Rachael's husband in custody while Smith had his little girl.

Oscar dialed Smith's number. "I've landed."

"Good. I'll text you the address of our rendezvous point, an abandoned building off Highway One-Thirty outside of San Jose. Aaron—er, Devlin—is claiming there's heroin there."

What did Aaron know about heroin?

"And the kid?"

"Your offspring's safe with me. I picked up a little something to keep her comfortable. And I got a US Marshal in the trunk."

"Is she dead?" Oscar felt a wave of nausea. His flight had been all of an hour and a half in the same state, so he couldn't claim the sensation was jet lag. He wouldn't be squeamish when it came to killing Aaron.

"Not yet. I didn't want to leave the body where it could be easily found. I mapped out this place we're headed to, and there's plenty of woods to dump a body."

Smith had wasted no time in assembling all the players and arranging a place to gather where they wouldn't be disturbed. Maybe it was better this way. Maybe Oscar didn't need time to contemplate all his options like his analytical lawyer's mind normally liked to do. He might waiver.

With Smith taking the lead, decisions would be made and action taken. As one of the West Coast's strong-arm satellites to the Gambino family, Smith possessed decisive qualities and was not in the least squeamish about pulling a trigger when needed. But Oscar knew, for this one, he would be the one to pull the trigger.

AUTUMN DROVE with focus down the highway. The US Marshal would already have a dozen officers on the lookout for Devlin's abductor. She could probably leave his kidnapping to the agency responsible for him. But she couldn't turn away knowing she could succeed where they might fail.

She had Devlin's crystal ball and Joy's help. As bizarre as that seemed, the ghost had alerted her to Devlin's abduction. Autumn may not understand this supernatural connection, but she respected it. She kept the crystal ball on the passenger seat and glanced at it from time to time.

A blue glow caught her eye. "Joy?"

Yes

The word floated in the crystal ball as if sprayed on the surface of a lake.

"What's Devlin's twenty? His location?" she clarified.

Soon

An image of a gas station, rippling and watery, materialized in the crystal ball.

"He's there?"

Yes

A liquid gray car came into view in the orb. The image zoomed into the trunk and then through the trunk where Devlin lay, barely visible in the dark.

"He's in the trunk. Okay." She ran a hand through her hair. "Is he injured?"

No

"Good. Great, actually. Thanks, Joy. Anything else I need to know?"

A series of images played through the crystal ball—Devlin younger by a few years with an infant in his arms against his bare chest, then pushing Kimmy as a toddler on a swing. In a ripple, the image transformed to him reading a book to his daughter in bed. Devlin's hair looked shorter, and he wore a trim facial hair, but his eyes were the same lovely green.

He was handsome. Handsome and sweet.

Autumn turned her focus back to the road. "He's a good dad, and you're worried about him. I get it. I can't watch home videos while I drive, though."

The images continued to play.

A few minutes later, Autumn spotted the gas station and slowed. A uniformed officer filled the gas tank of a gray Charger. Autumn pulled around and parked on the far side of the convenience store. There were two other bystanders filling their tanks. She couldn't risk pulling her weapon and forcing the cop into a deadly standoff. Also, there wasn't time to call Marshal Williams and wait for her to bring the cavalry.

When the kidnapper finished fueling, he replaced the nozzle and walked into the store. Autumn eased out of her car in a heartbeat, leaving the engine running and dashing to the Charger. She bent behind the driver's side door, opened it, and popped the trunk.

Before she reached the back of the vehicle, Devlin was already struggling to climb out with his hands cuffed together in front of him. When she helped him out the rest of the way, half blind from the light and stumbling, he didn't startle at her touch, so she suspected Joy had told him she'd arrived.

"Stay low," Autumn commanded as she reached up and closed the trunk. With any luck, the cop would drive away, thinking Devlin was still inside his car.

Together, they scurried in a crouch, trying to stay lower than the window-level view from the convenience store. Autumn watched the store, hoping the door would remain closed.

She didn't want to take the time to shuffle around her car, so she helped Devlin into the backseat before climbing into the driver's seat.

As she reversed the car, a shot rang out, and her side view mirror shattered. Autumn floored the pedal, jumping the curb into the parking lot of a fast food restaurant. She spun the car before slamming it into drive.

She jerked the car right, and her wheels connected back with Highway 99. Glancing into the back seat, she saw Devlin hunkered low.

"Are you okay?" she asked.

He lifted his head. "Yeah. I'm okay. You?"

She nodded, strapping herself in. "I'm fine."

Struggling and grunting, Devlin climbed into the passenger seat beside her with his hands still cuffed in front of him. Autumn moved the crystal ball out of his way and into her lap. He brushed against her as he settled into the seat and pulled his seatbelt into place.

"I can't believe you came for me." His voice sounded breathless from the exertion and the excitement.

She tugged long, feathery strands of hair out of her face. "Well, I've never taken orders from a ghost before, so that's an unforgettable experience. I don't suppose Joy would be willing to become an FBI consultant? Help us catch bad guys from time to time?"

Devlin's lips curled in a grin. "You want to be the crazy agent who carries a crystal ball around with her?" He didn't let her answer before continuing. "When Joy told me you'd found me and you were about to open the trunk... oh, the relief."

When he reached over and took the crystal ball from her, Autumn noticed his wrists were chafed and red from the cuffs.

She ran a finger along the edge of the raw skin. "We've got to get you out of those bracelets."

He gripped her hand and turned a pair of intense green eyes on her. "Thank you for rescuing me."

Autumn turned her attention back to the road, stifling the surprise rush of heat at his touch and his stare. Fortunately, she was driving and her hands were occupied because she had an irrational desire to crawl into his lap, and not because he looked vulnerable—he'd proven his resilience, keeping his wits first in an assassination then in being kidnapped—but because she felt vulnerable.

She never felt vulnerable.

But in the moments before she'd reached him, she'd feared losing him. She wanted to know him—this fascinating and determined father who had relationships with ghosts. She'd rescued him only to have to hand him over to an organization that would sweep him away somewhere she couldn't reach him.

She left her hand in his while they drove, until she could think of something to say that wasn't as ridiculous as, "Can I see you again sometime?"

After several minutes, Autumn pulled her hand back and pulled off the main highway. After a series of turns, she pulled around to the back side of a shopping center, not visible from the road.

"Let's see those hands." Autumn withdrew her lock-pick set and worked on his cuffs.

"You can pick locks?"

"I chase thieves for a leaving. Need to know how they work."

"Can you crack safes, too."

She gave him a mischevious grin.

When his hands were free, Devlin rubbed his wrists. "Thank you."

She stayed leaning toward him, recalling the bare-chested image Joy had shown her. What did those lips taste like, and why did she ache to know? Had she learned nothing from her cheating fiancé? Was she going to wear her attraction openly for Devlin to see?

He started to lean forward when Autumn's phone rang. She pulled it out of her jacket pocket.

"It's Harriet."

Harriet probably wanted the reassurance of hearing Devlin's voice rather than Autumn's, so she handed the phone to him.

DEVLIN TOOK THE PHONE, cooling his fervor. He'd wanted to kiss Autumn more than he wanted his next breath. Her long hair caught the light of the setting sun and looked radiant. She smelled of honeysuckle.

And her golden eyes had been brimming with desire. Had Joy been working her matchmaking mojo on Autumn?

Devlin held the phone to his ear. "Harriet." He wanted to hear Kimmy's voice. Although he'd been with her just an hour ago, many terrible events had transpired since then.

"US Marshal Williams can't come to the phone right now."

Devlin's stomach hit rock bottom. "Oscar." He hadn't heard that voice in six years, but he recognized it instantly.

Autumn's head jerked in his direction.

Devlin's world tilted on its axis, and he gripped the dash to steady himself. If Oscar had Harriet's phone and Harriet, then he had Kimmy, too.

"Aaron, is that you?" Oscar asked, his coy tone suggesting he already knew Devlin was on the other end of the line.

Devlin's throat constricted. No one had called him that name since he'd gone into witness protection. With shaking hands, he put the phone on speaker and set it down on the console of the car.

"Where's Kimmy?" He hated how pleading his voice sounded. His tone conveyed that he'd be willing to give Oscar whatever he wanted for Kimmy's safe return.

"You didn't tell me I had a daughter."

Devlin's mind raced back to the timing of the conversation with the cop. Mazzone had promised not to tell Oscar about Kimmy if Devlin obeyed, but since Kimmy was in Oscar's custody so soon, the cop had evidently already told him.

"Daddy?"

Devlin threw a hand over his mouth to keep from screaming at the sound of Kimmy's frightened, tentative voice. Red waves swam before his vision as his temples throbbed.

A firm hand cupped his face. Then two. Devlin looked into Autumn's liquid amber eyes as her touch grounded him.

You can do this, she mouthed.

He nodded and lowered his hands. Autumn clasped them in her own.

"Hi, sweetie," Devlin said into the phone, trying to keep the fear out of his voice.

"I want to go home."

"I know, Kimmy. I'm coming to get you."

"Aaron," Oscar's voice came back to the forefront. "Your abductor told the guy I answer to that you know the whereabouts of a stash of heroin. He wants to meet there."

Of course he does.

"What happens when I do?" Devlin's voice hardened— he felt as if Autumn was infusing strength into him.

"We have a conversation. But you have to come alone."

"You swear to me right now that Kimmy remains unharmed, no matter what happens."

"I'm not going to injure my own child. I'm not a monster."

Oh, but he was, Devlin knew. Even though he'd loved Rachael, he'd barely hesitated shooting her when she and Devlin were escaping. And he'd sworn he would kill Devlin, too.

How much darker had Oscar sunk after six years of living in hiding? How many times would he have plotted in his mind the ways to kill him?

"I'll be there." Devlin ended the call.

CHAPTER 9

*A*s Devlin stared at the black screen of the phone, the car seemed to close around him. He had a sudden, demanding need for air. Thrashing, he found the handle and shoved the passenger door open. He stumbled out before falling to his knees.

Not Kimmy.

Everything Devlin had built to keep Kimmy safe had crumbled in a matter of hours. As he knelt on the asphalt, clutching his stomach, he felt spirits converging. His anguish was summoning them.

Autumn stood a few feet from him, her hair whipped around in the frenzied disturbance created by the ghosts.

Murmurs and whispers rushed around him—so much suffering. Sometimes the anguished ghosts were drawn like magnets to the suffering of the living, especially since the veil between the spirit world and the world of flesh thinned on All Hallows' Eve.

"Leave me!" Devlin commanded. He couldn't help any

of them right now. He needed to help himself, to pull himself together.

Gentle arms wrapped around him, pulling him to his feet and into safety. Autumn held him, stroking his hair. Her face was so close, he could feel the warmth of her breath.

"We'll get her back, Devlin."

He sniffed and took a shuddering exhalation. "Damn right we will."

Devlin tried to take a step back, but Autumn kept her hold on him.

"Just take a moment. Take a moment to breathe."

Devlin relaxed in her embrace as his arms wrapped around her narrow waist. He hadn't embraced another woman since Racheal.

After a few steadying breaths, he looked down at her. "I'm okay."

Autumn moved her hands to his face, brushing against his short facial hair. Compassionate eyes bore into his soul. She stretched up to him and pressed her lips to his. Devlin startled from a combination of surprise at her boldness and shock at his body's heated reaction.

She stepped back, running a hand through her hair. "Damn, I'm sorry. That was completely uncalled for."

He closed the gap between them, bent down, and kissed her. His hands moved from her jaw around to her neck before he crushed his body against hers and devoured her in a heated kiss. Autumn released a moan, causing him to back her against the car as he fisted her hair and deepened the kiss.

When he broke away, they were both breathless. His

heated yet worried eyes scanned her expression. She smiled as if to let him know she'd enjoyed it and had no regrets.

She licked her lips. "Why don't we process that later? Let's get Kimmy back."

Devlin nodded.

"Is she Oscar's?" Her voice sounded gentle.

"No." He turned and leaned against the car. "She's mine. But it's just like the arrogant prick to assume he's the father. I'm not going to correct him if it means he's less likely to hurt Kimmy, thinking she's his."

He shoved his hands into his pockets. "Rachael and I were married when she took the junior associate position with Oscar's law firm—later discovered to be one of the firms in the pocket of the Gambino crime family. She confessed an affair with Oscar at the same time she told me what she'd discovered of the firm's illegal activities. We plotted for months on how to safely disassociate ourselves. By the time our plan matured to fruition and we'd saved enough money to flee, Rachael was thirty-four weeks pregnant."

Rubbing his neck and pacing, Devlin continued. "Oscar discovered us loading the car. He'd come over to confess his love and ask why she'd shut him out for months. They fought, and she started to go into labor. In a fit of rage, he fired at me." Devlin shook his head. "It should've been me, but Rachael shoved me out of the way and the bullet hit her. I dragged her to the car, and we were able to escape because Oscar had a meltdown at having shot the woman he claimed to love. But I didn't get her to the hospital in time to save her life."

His head spun from the combination of worry, hunger, and anguish of reliving that night.

"Rachael stayed with me as a ghost. She's the reason I lived—guiding me to the trustworthy cops, then FBI, and eventually Harriet. When Kimmy turned one, Rachael moved on. Told me I needed to move on also. Kimmy and I were safe."

Finally telling someone the entire story felt cathartic. A weight lifted off Devlin. "Thanks for listening."

"Thank you for sharing that with me." Autumn rubbed a soothing hand along his biceps. "Now, let's get Kimmy back." When her smile blossomed, it nearly took his breath away.

He nodded and climbed back into the passenger seat.

Autumn sat in the driver's seat and situated the vehicle headed west. "What did you do back there with the wind?"

"My nervous breakdown in the parking lot?"

"Something supernatural was happening. Leaves started spinning around you. Was it Joy?"

"It was my anguish—not a person, just the emotion. My suffering drew spirits to me."

"Do you do that often?"

"That's a first for me. I think because it's Halloween and the division between our world and the spirit world is more of a thin waterfall than a solid wall right now."

"So you were telling them to leave, not me?"

"Oh, God yes. You can't leave. I can't do this without you."

The corners of her lips curved upward at his declaration. "Have you ever summoned ghosts like that for a customer?"

"No. Sometimes lights flicker or candle flames dance, but usually the crystal ball is sufficient. I don't like so many at once. They make me cold and claustrophobic. I'm actually surprised you didn't run away screaming."

"It felt and looked disconcerting, but I don't run screaming from anything. Also, I trusted that whatever you were doing, you had enough control not to let it hurt me."

"I'd never do anything to hurt you." He stared out the window, watching a great silver moon rise above the tree line. He realized, if he was going to pull off the rescue of his daughter, he would have to cast off his inhibitions and be prepared to call an army of ghosts to his side.

OSCAR DROPPED the phone back into his pocket. Aaron would show.

Turning, Oscar eyed the abandoned building with a scowl. Well, they certainly wouldn't be bothered on Halloween night in a place like this. And with the surrounding woods, no one would hear gunshots. If they left Rachael's husband's body here, he might never be found.

Smith handed Oscar a gun. "There's only one man standing between you and your freedom."

"I want my job and my life back," Oscar grumbled.

From Oscar's position—a foot taller than Smith—he could see the man's bald patch on the top of his head.

Smith was short and stocky, but Oscar knew him to be a competent thug for the Gambino family.

"So we're clear. If I do this—if I eliminate Aaron—I get back into the Gambino family. I get my job back in Chicago."

"Yes. You go back to being an overpaid lawyer in a penthouse working for the Gambinos." Smith looked around at the surroundings. "I hate spooky shit like this."

"This place?"

"It doesn't creep you out?"

Oscar arched an eyebrow. "It's just a building." He wasn't 'creeped out' so much as turned off by the grime and cobwebs.

Smith spit on the ground. "My grandmother always swore she saw ghosts. She always said that if you did evil deeds, the spirits would eventually come for you. What are you smirking at?"

"I didn't take you to be the superstitious type."

"You don't feel anything here? Especially on Halloween?"

"Feel what?" Oscar asked.

"The chill. The hair on the back of your neck standing up."

"I'm more worried about getting dust on my suit than stirring up ghosts and goblins."

Officer Mazzone emerged from inside the building. "It's a nice stash of heroin. Nobody would think to check an abandoned building like this. One of my guys learned that some DEA agents got wind of the transport truck's plates, so the truck driver had to stash it and lay low while he found new transportation. Word on the street is only Cesar Torres's men know this cash cow is here, and some of them will be here in the morning to pick it up to take it north."

"Then I guess we'd better move it before morning," Smith said. "We don't want Torres to know we took it. We'll finish up our business here and then load it into our trunks."

Oscar would let these two men handle the heroin. He had no interest in drugs, and he had no doubt Smith knew who in the Gambino crime family would be capable of turning the stolen narcotics into cash.

Mazzone sized up the cars parked in the lot. "It should all fit between the two vehicles."

A thumping noise came from Smith's trunk.

"Guess the US Marshal's awake," Smith said with a snort. "She was a handful to subdue, but I caught her off guard."

"What do we do with her?" Oscar asked.

"We'll finish her off after Aaron."

"What about the girl?"

"I imagine after you run a paternity test, she'll be yours."

Oscar glanced at the girl in the back seat, who watched the two men with tears in her eyes and clutched the stuffed animal Smith had picked up for her when he'd bought diphenhydramine to sedate her. She looked so much like Rachael. Big green eyes stared at him. Was she his? She must be.

"She'll be asleep soon," Smith said. "When she is, we'll canvas the building and pick a place to confront our expected guests." He shivered one last time as he looked at the building.

~

AUTUMN GLANCED at Devlin as he stared out the car window. The light of the moon outlined his handsome features.

She was driving a man who could talk to ghosts to meet a criminal of the Gambino crime family who held his daughter hostage. The entire situation defied comprehension but wasn't beyond belief—not since she'd now seen ghostly activity several times for herself.

To compound the extraordinary, she had feelings for Devlin. Something had sprouted in the short time they'd spent together and had manifested as a spontaneous kiss. And that was no tentative first kiss. She'd had first kisses —timid ones, exploratory ones, delicate ones. The electric and sizzling kiss she'd shared with him had been unbelievable.

Devlin Angelo.

Maybe he was an angel. His kiss made her feel like she'd been lifted to heaven. It drove away the pain she'd been harboring from her cheating fiancé.

But now wasn't the time to explore their brief sensual experience. They needed to get Devlin's daughter back to the safety of her father.

"I hope Harriet is okay. God. I didn't even ask about her." Devlin rubbed his temple.

Autumn reached out and held his hand. "Hey. Hey. One thing at a time. Let's focus on getting Kimmy back."

She hesitated a beat, watching as they zoomed past the next mile marker. "We'd have a lot of backup if I call for reinforcements." Even as Autumn made the suggestion, she knew Devlin would decline.

"No." He shook his head. He tried to withdraw his hand, but she refused to let it go. He added, "I'm not risking Kimmy."

"Okay, Devlin. No backup. But I'm not sitting on the sidelines. Our plan needs to include me."

"I had time in the trunk of the car to ponder options. I think I can get a different type of reinforcement."

Autumn shot him a sidelong glance. Was he suggesting what she thought he was suggesting?

"Let's talk it through," she said. "Oscar wants you because you're the only one who can testify against him."

"Yes. I'm the key to the prosecution's case against his shooting Rachael."

"And he's also angry with you because he thinks Kimmy is his child—a child he's been estranged from for six years. A child he's using as bait."

"Yes."

"And does Oscar have any reason to want to keep you alive?"

"No."

She rolled her shoulders, feeling the reassuring weight of her loaded gun. Oscar had many reasons to be pissed at Devlin. "I'm not seeing how this rendezvous ends well for you."

Autumn let the silence settle as she watched Devlin's worried expression.

"He's the criminal," Devlin shot back.

Autumn grinned slightly at his spunk. "I understand that. I'm just analyzing the situation from the criminal's perspective." Her voice tightened. "And I don't like your odds. Trading yourself for Kimmy is not a solution. You can't leave her fatherless. I own a backup gun, but do you even know how to use a gun?"

Devlin shook his head.

"Well, the dirty cop will probably be there, so it's not as though you can shoot your way out. We'll have to figure out how I can sneak in and become the element of surprise. What? Why are you grinning?"

"I should probably be curled up in a ball crying, but to hear you worried on my behalf, well, I haven't had that from anyone in a long time. It's nice."

The way he'd hesitated over the word "anyone," Autumn suspected he'd almost said "woman." She'd never read the WITSEC contract, but she was sure it didn't demand celibacy. Perhaps he'd cautiously avoided relationships due to his experience with Rachael cheating. Perhaps he was protecting Kimmy.

"I am worried about you, and, short of locking you up, I don't think I can keep you from trying to save Kimmy."

Devlin arched an eyebrow on an otherwise stern face, conveying that the fiery depths of hell wouldn't keep him from Kimmy.

"Right," Autumn continued. "So, I want a plan that doesn't involve endangering you to get Kimmy back."

"There is no such plan, Special Agent Bentley. I have to go inside that building looking like I'm alone."

"You're not alone." Still holding his hand, she squeezed.

He gripped her right hand as she drove. Turning it palm up, he ran a delicate finger along the lines, sending a shudder of desire through her.

"Do you read palms in addition to seeing ghosts?" Autumn asked.

"I had to learn. I don't really want people thinking I'm reading their future, but they think I'm a charlatan if I don't read palms in addition to see ghosts while claiming to be a psychic."

Autumn chuckled. "Humor me." Her voice sounded a little husky, and she hoped he hadn't noticed. The longer he stared at her hand, the longer she enjoyed the pleasure of his touch. Yet, having him focus on palm reading also distracted him from the stress of what was to come.

Devlin traced the edge of her palm. "You have a square hand, which suggests you are practical, organized, and persistent."

"And all this time I thought I needed to wear a suit to convey that."

He chuckled before continuing, "The left hand is for the future. The right hand is for the past. Your three main lines are strong—heart, head, and life. Your heart line begins below your index finger, so you are, or will be, content in love. It's also very straight, suggesting a good handle on emotions. It's not wavy to suggest a plethora of superficial lovers. A small line crossing through here suggests trauma."

She shifted in her seat.

"Now, your head line doesn't join your life line."

"Is that good or bad?"

"It means you're adventurous." He winked at her. "But

it's also deep, so you're a clear, focused thinker." Devlin ran a finger from midway between her index finger and thumb down toward her wrist.

She resisted the urge to suck in a deep breath and betray how tantalizing his touch felt to her.

"Your life line curves nicely—plenty of energy. And it's deep, suggesting vitality."

He looked up at her with wide eyes and a pleasant grin.

Swallowing, she said, "Whatever you charge to do that isn't enough."

"You're the only person I've touched that tenderly while doing a reading."

"I'm honored." She groaned inwardly. Apparently, her brain had taken a hiatus, leaving her with lame words.

Devlin grinned, lifted her palm to his lips, and pressed a kiss into her hand.

He took a deep breath. "Okay. I have a plan to get Kimmy back. We're going to need Joy to give us a detailed layout of the rendezvous building."

CHAPTER 10

*D*evlin climbed out of Autumn's car and walked to the driver's side. He towered over her in a close, protective fashion before she could leave. Behind her, a full moon lit the sky, growing more magnificent as the dusk sky darkened.

"Listen, Autumn."

"No goodbyes. We've got a good plan."

He pursed his lips. "When Rachael told me about Oscar, we should have gone to the police. We didn't know who to trust. Maybe if I'd found a ghost to guide us, then things would have turned out differently. I carry a lot of guilt about how I handled things. Anyway, life spiraled out of control. Each time I replay the shooting in my mind, I see Oscar's face—almost as terrified as we were. Rachael's ghost later told me that was the first time he'd killed someone."

Autumn's jaw tensed, and she started to open her mouth.

"I'm not making excuses for him. He's an animal and a murderer. I guess I'm making excuses for myself."

Autumn shook her head. "I'm not judging you, Devlin. But you need to remember that the man you knew six years ago isn't the same man you're going to stare down tonight in that abandoned building. Maybe he wasn't prone to violence and was caught in a jealous rage that night, and maybe he'd made a series of bad decisions. But he's been a wanted murderer for six years, and there's no telling what he's become or who else he's put a bullet into in order to stay hidden all this time."

Devlin blew out a breath as he nodded, respecting and appreciating her insight.

Autumn cupped his chin and ran a thumb along his jaw. "I've got your back, Angelo."

He grinned. "Who's the guardian angel in this scenario?"

"We'll guard each other."

He gripped her shoulders. "I know."

Her breath hitched as she stared into his vibrant eyes, but neither she nor Devlin moved closer to each other.

He stepped aside, giving Autumn space to leave as he situated himself in the driver's seat of the car.

"I'll see you soon." Autumn took off at a trot under cover of darkness.

Devlin pulled the door shut before putting the vehicle in drive.

Joy appeared beside him, sitting in the passenger seat. "Oh, honey, that kiss after you found out about Kimmy was more delightful than fried chicken wrapped in a waffle topped with hot maple syrup."

"That's a thing? Fried chicken and waffles?"

"Sure is. You haven't lived until you've had Southern-style chicken and waffles. Don't forget the fixings—pancake syrup, bourbon, and salted butter. Mouth-watering good!"

Devlin chuckled.

"Hey, you didn't kiss that little filly just now when she left."

Devlin frowned. "It would have felt too much like a goodbye kiss. Anyway, are we ready at the asylum?"

When Devlin took the next right, the psychiatric hospital came into view.

"I reckon we're ready," Joy confirmed.

The three-story structure was made of red brick partially covered in creeping vines. Oversized, paned windows, thick with grime, loomed on every floor. In daylight, it probably had an unassuming blandness. Tonight, bathed in watery moonlight and surrounded by twisted trees that had already shed their leaves, it looked diabolical.

Genius plan. Rendezvous in a spooky building on Halloween. Well, it was Oscar's mistake.

"What about Cesar Torres or any of his men showing up tonight?" Devlin didn't want another layer of complexity.

"Not tonight. They have plans to move the heroin stash tomorrow."

As Devlin parked the car beside two other cars, he recognized the Charger belonging to metal mouth Officer Mazzone. Oscar wasn't alone.

No matter.

Neither was he.

Devlin walked to the building and pushed open the door. "Oscar?" He announced his arrival. Quietly, to Joy floating beside him, he added, "Where are they?"

"First floor. They found the heroin art in a closet."

Devlin peered down a long, dark corridor. Light flickered from the entrance of a room in the distance. As he followed the glow, Joy added, "The dirty cop is coming up behind you."

Devlin raised his hands so Mazzone could see he was unarmed. Although, he wasn't helpless anymore. But Mazzone didn't know that.

A flashlight flickered on behind him.

"Keep walking."

"Did you find the heroin as promised?" Devlin asked.

"It's a pretty stash."

In a low murmur, Devlin began his chant.

"I beckon thee
    Rise and be still
    Come to me
    Heed my will.

By stars and stones
    From rest uncoil
    By moonlight shone
    Bid do my toil."

"What'd you say?" asked Mazonne.

"Nervous mumbling."

Devlin quietly continued. Feeling the presence of

spirits assembling as he laced his words with all the worry and pain and suffering he'd ever experienced.

"Knock it off," the cop growled.

When Devlin reached the large room on the right, a bright moon shone through an expansive wall of windows. This had been the cafeteria, according to Joy's detailed layout of the place. There were no tables now, only one large chamber with two exit points and a set of doors leading to the kitchen. Layers of dust and grime covered the floors and filled the corners of the room.

Oscar stood at one end, and at his feet lay a small ball. Devlin's heart leapt into his throat. When he tried to step forward, Mazzone yanked him back by his shirt collar.

"What have you done to Kimmy?"

"Over-the-counter sedative. She's fine. I'm not a monster, Aaron."

Devlin turned his steely glare on Oscar. The lawyer had changed his appearance—silicone implants to enhance his cheeks and a hairline that had receded substantially over the years. His build was still thin but looked almost gaunt now.

A man Devlin didn't recognize stood next to Oscar. He was short and stout with rosacea lines on his wrinkled face. A bulge under his leather jacket betrayed the presence of a weapon. His dark eyes looked like lumps of cold, lifeless coal. Oscar may claim not to be a monster, but this man certainly was one.

"Where's Harriet?"

"Alive. For now."

"Oscar, you have millions in heroin. Just take the stash and go. Leave Kimmy and me here."

"You were never going to tell me I was a father?"

"You're a criminal. I had to protect her."

"Are we done with the reunion?" the short man asked. "It's all very touching, but you're only alive until we know if you have some evidence beyond your eyewitness testimony."

"Who are you?" Devlin asked.

"Oscar's protection. My name is Smith, and you and Rachel mucked things up. Cost us a lot of money."

Devlin stared at Oscar as the lawyer raised a gun.

Oscar hesitated. "Is she mine?"

Devlin grit his teeth, clenched his fist, and forced command into his words. "Spirits come to me. Heed my will."

His breath curled in white wisps as the temperature in the room plummeted.

AUTUMN NAVIGATED by the light of the moon through the woods and toward the abandoned psychiatric hospital. She hadn't liked Devlin's plan—him entering alone and unarmed, but Devlin had logically refuted all the proposals Autumn had countered with. That left her dashing through the woods, thanking the full moon for lighting her way, and hoping not to encounter any headless horseman... because that was just the type of day she was having.

As promised by Joy, the back door was unlocked. She eased it open enough to slip inside, cringing as rusted hinges slightly creaked.

Silently, leading with her Glock, Autumn followed the murmur of voices to the cafeteria, which she knew from Devlin's description had two entry points, plus a third through the food preparation area. Light from the full moon barely penetrated the smeared paned windows with their grim iron bars, but it was enough to prevent her from running into any walls.

Once Devlin had driven away and Autumn was out of sight, she'd called the FBI office for reinforcements. She'd promised Devlin she wouldn't take action that might endanger Kimmy, and she wouldn't. By the time the team arrived, Devlin would have had his confrontation with Oscar and Autumn would have gotten Kimmy to safety. But she needed to have a team there afterward to keep the villains contained.

Once inside the kitchen, Autumn snaked around countertops, following the sound of voices. When she peered through the small circular window on a door separating the kitchen from the cafeteria, her stomach clenched.

The cop who'd kidnapped Devlin stood behind him, holding a gun to his back. Two men facing Devlin had their backs to the door. Three against one.

But Kimmy. Where was Kimmy?

There. Curled in a ball, sleeping on the floor with a blanket for a pillow.

Autumn stifled her urge to race to Devlin's rescue, recalling her conversation with him in the car.

"Your first objective is getting Kimmy to safety."

"I'm not abandoning you."

"You'd better not come for me until Kimmy is safe."

"So, I'm to pull a snatch-and-grab while the scheming villain gives his monologue?" Autumn had questioned the validity of Devlin's plan.

"You'll have a signal."

"What signal?"

"You'll know it when you feel it," he'd said.

Feel it.

As promised, Autumn felt something like cold tentacles and a brief submersion in frigid water that left her a bit breathless. She eased the door open as thick, dark clouds covered the moon and plunged the room into darkness. The cop's flashlight flickered out.

The room erupted in panicked shouts, but Autumn kept steady pursuit of her objective as she scooped up Kimmy's warm little body. She slunk back behind the kitchen door, carrying the sleeping child.

DEVLIN SHIVERED, partly from the cold and partly from fear. Was he out of his mind summoning so many spirits? And ones dwelling in an abandoned asylum no less. Troubled spirits. Tortured spirits.

Yet, from what he knew of ghosts, they couldn't physically harm anyone, and none of them were outright evil. They could cause a fright, which might be harmful to someone in a hazardous environment—a forest, stairs, or dark, abandoned buildings—or to someone with a heart condition. But by and large they weren't malicious and often wanted to help and feel a connection to the living.

Devlin had never attempted to demand help from so

many, but he'd never been in a situation where his daughter was in danger.

"What the hell is happening?" Oscar snapped.

Spirits flooded into the room, spiraling and filling the space. Like a miniature, magical tornado, they stirred the air, whipping up dust and disrupting the battery-powered flashlight.

Devlin was the only one who could see the spirits, so while others felt the wind blowing past them and heard rattling windows, Devlin could see their gray, navy, white, and gold brilliance. Outside, the clouds blanketed the moon, and all was submerged in darkness.

He used the distraction to drop to the floor and sweep a leg out wide. He struck Mazzone's knee with a crack, and the cop screamed and fell onto his back.

Devlin rolled toward the hallway. When he sprang to his feet, Joy hovered by the exit, lighting Devlin's escape route.

"Aaron!" Oscar called into the dark void. "What's going on? Smith, the girl is missing!"

Devlin smirked, even as he ran for the exit. Autumn had succeeded. Wonder Woman she was indeed—she'd gathered Kimmy in her arms and whisked her to safety.

Devlin ran down the corridor, trusting the streaks of light along the floor that Joy had created. She was saving his life.

"Oh, honey. You've gone and done it now! You made those men madder than hornets on fire."

When Devlin reached the front doors, he grasped the handle with both hands. It didn't budge.

Damn!

The cop must have locked it behind him.

From the cafeteria, a flashlight emerged, sweeping in his direction. He didn't have time to fumble for the lock in the dark or to ask Joy to show him where it was. He spun and sprinted toward the back of the building.

"Joy," Devlin gasped between breaths. "I need an alternate exit."

"I'll guide the way, but I sure as hell can't make you bulletproof."

A shot rang out.

CHAPTER 11

*A*utumn's blood ran cold when she heard a gunshot. As she laid Kimmy down in the back seat of her car, the girl looked at her groggily and smiled.

"Autumn."

She gave the girl a strained smile. Kimmy might never smile at her again if she didn't save her father.

Several vehicles pulled into the dilapidated parking lot. Autumn pulled out her identification and held it up as two men and two women approached.

The woman in the lead wore a suit, and her hair was pulled into a severe blonde ponytail. She held up her own ID—Special Agent Marks—as she glanced around at the building and grounds. "You called this in?"

"Autumn Bentley." She spoke quickly, needing to brief them but wanting to run back inside to help Devlin get to safety. "There are three male perps, armed, and one civilian man inside. This is his daughter. There are two entry and exit points. The one you see and the one on the south side." Autumn reached into the car and grasped the crystal ball, then turned with a jerk.

"Whoa. Where are you going?" Marks laid a hand on her forearm.

"Shots fired. I need to get back in there."

"You, with no vest and a crystal ball? You have a team, Special Agent Bentley. Let's coordinate this." She nodded to one of her men, who handed Autumn a spare bullet-proof vest.

Autumn pursed her lips before nodding. As she donned the vest, she spoke. "You two cover the rear." She pointed to the two male agents. "Anyone who comes out of that building gets arrested. You," she turned to the non-lead female, "guard the door and guard the child. Nothing happens to her."

"Is she injured?"

Autumn shook her head. "Sleeping."

She turned toward Agent Marks. "You and I through the front."

"Lead the way." Marks took her gun from her holster, and the other agents followed suit.

The two men peeled off around the back of the building. Overhead, the clouds parted from the moon. Autumn hoped the passing clouds indicated Devlin no longer needed help from the spirits, and not that he wasn't alive to keep them summoned.

As she and the agent crouched on either side of the door, Autumn glanced at Special Agent Marks. She appreciated her unquestioning cooperation, even if she didn't understand what she'd done to deserve it.

She nodded her readiness as she reached for the door.

Locked!

The hinges opened outward, so it wasn't as though she could kick the door down—not that the heavy oak would do anything other than scoff at attempts to make it yield.

She set her gun and crystal ball down, patted down her pockets, and withdrew her lock picks. "Light."

Marks held up her phone flashlight as Autumn worked steadily to pick the lock. She felt the spring give way. As she turned the handle, the old door creaked open. She pocketed her picks, retrieved her gun and orb, and crept inside the building.

Autumn strained to listen over the sound of her blood pumping like a freight train through her ears. She suppressed the urge to call to Devlin. She looked down both corridors, to the right and left. Nothing.

Lifting the orb in her hand, she asked, "Joy, where's Devlin?" Autumn ignored the FBI agent staring at her like she'd sprouted a horn.

The crystal ball glowed blue as a white arrow appeared, pointing downward.

"Down. The basement?"

A liquid "yes" appeared in reply.

"A crystal ball? Is that how you solved the Ying case?" Marks asked.

Autumn followed the directions Joy gave her to find the stairs to the basement. "No. This contraption is an entirely new technique."

So, the Ying case. Autumn's reputation from that circus had earned her Marks's team's immediate cooperation for tonight's endeavor. At least some good had come from the hype of the Ying case.

"FBI! Hands in the air!" Special Agent Marks had spotted the man a second before Autumn.

The man, wearing khakis and a polo shirt, threw up his arms. No gun. Autumn recognized him from the cafeteria as the man who'd stood beside Oscar.

"Get me out of here. Just get me out of here. There's something wrong with this place! I haven't hurt anyone," he said.

His face looked pale, and Autumn resisted the urge to ask him if he'd seen a ghost.

As Marks cuffed him, Autumn kept walking toward the stairs.

"Where's Oscar? Where's Aaron?" The man's questions emerged in rapid fire.

Devlin. He'd always be Devlin to Autumn.

"Special Agent Bentley," Marks called after her, "give me a minute. I'll pass this guy off and guard your flank."

The crystal ball had transitioned from a gentle glowing blue to a pulsing strobe light.

"I don't think I have a minute to waste."

DEVLIN HAD no control over his heart as it pounded like a stampede of cattle. Ugh, now his internal monologue sounded like Joy.

It was only a matter of time before Oscar found his current hiding spot. Oscar must have retrieved Mazzone's flashlight or had one of his own. And he'd managed to keep his cool when ghosts were wreaking havoc.

Devlin hunkered down behind a large rolling bin designed for dirty clothes. His ankle and elbow throbbed with dull pain where he'd banged his body as he tumbled down the laundry chute to the basement level. It had been his only means of escape when Oscar had fired at him and he'd sought cover in a utility room.

Oscar hadn't followed him down the chute, but he'd deduced its destination and now lurked in the basement by the sound of his loafers lightly crunching on a soft layer of dirt and dust coating the floor.

Slow, deliberate, stalking steps.

Hells bells! Devlin swore. Why couldn't Oscar take the heroin and run?

Because he doesn't have the sense God gave a goose. Well, damn, Devlin was sounding like Joy again.

The footsteps grew closer.

Regardless of what happened to him, Kimmy was safe. Autumn had taken her to safety, and that was all that mattered.

A bright white light from Oscar's flashlight pierced inside the room where Devlin crouched. He shrunk back. His last bag of tricks—chanting for spirits—wouldn't work this time. Oscar would hear him and fill him with lead before the ghosts could come to his rescue.

The footsteps stopped as the light panned across the floor of the room.

Crap! Crap! Crap!

Oscar would see Devlin's footprints leading to the bin.

"FBI! Drop your weapon!"

Autumn!

Devlin hazarded a glance over the bin. Oscar began turning as if intending to fire his weapon at Autumn.

Not on my watch!

Gripping the heavy, decrepit bin, Devlin pushed with all his might. It crashed into Oscar, hurling him off balance and sending him into the wall with a cry of surprise and pain. The impact sent the weapon and flashlight flying. The room and hallway went dark except for a faint blue glow.

Two figures wrestled in the corridor, grunting and punching. Devlin eased past the bin and picked up the gun. He couldn't tell who was winning, but he was prepared to shoot Oscar if he bested Autumn.

The light from the orb grew brighter, enabling Devlin to see the action in the hallway more clearly. With a last series of punches, Oscar crumpled to the ground. Autumn slapped cuffs on his wrist before taking a step back to catch her breath.

Devlin lowered the gun he'd had trained on Oscar. He peered at Autumn through the dim azure light. He couldn't tell if she was injured, but at least she was standing.

"Are you okay?" he asked, lowering the gun.

In three quick strides, she stood in front of him, taking the gun and slipping her hands around his waist. He dipped his head and kissed her—deep and sensuous. Every part of his body felt simultaneously light as a feather and grounded solidly in her. She moved her hands along his back. He stroked a hand over her hair.

"You tell me," she said, pulling him tight to her.

"Yeah, you're okay."

"I heard that gunshot, and it scared the hell out of me," Autumn said.

"You and me both. I think Joy even leaked a little ectoplasm."

Autumn chuckled.

"Besides," Devlin said, "you can't die. I don't need another ghost in my life." He glanced at Oscar. "Or skeletons."

"You turned out to be my angel after all. He would've shot me."

He kissed her forehead. "Part angel, part devil. But only in ways you might like."

She laughed. "I suspect you may be right."

AUTUMN GLANCED at Devlin in the back seat of her car as the parking lot of the abandoned psychiatric ward was bathed in blue and red flashing lights.

While Special Agent Marks had apprehended the mobster helping Oscar, and Autumn had made her way to the basement, the dirty cop had tried to flee via the back door, where the two FBI agents had waited. Now all the men who'd been after Devlin were in police custody.

Marks's team had found twenty-five kilograms of heroin disguised as art on canvas stashed exactly where Joy had said it would be.

Police were still securing the scene, and Autumn would have to give her statement to the police after Marks had finished with her questioning. Not to mention, Autumn still had to write her own detailed report. Her case was closed. California border control had tipped her off about the possible forged art, and her investigation had led her to a sizable heroin bust. She'd probably get some ridiculous amount of credit for it—like the Ying case—when she was just doing her job.

Yet, the best part of this investigation was that it had led her to Devlin.

"Special Agent Bentley?"

"Yes, sorry. Where were we?"

"How did you find Mr. Angelo after Officer Mazzone kidnapped him?"

Autumn frowned. She glanced at the quiescent globe in her car. Saying "a ghost told me" would destroy her credibility, but she also didn't want to lie.

"Bentley?"

"A hunch." She ran a hand through her hair.

Special Agent Marks arched an eyebrow, looking up from her notebook. She followed Autumn's gaze to the car before turning back to her. "You want me to write that you followed a crystal ball?"

"Um. No."

Marks sighed. "Okay. What do you want on the record?"

"Tracking device." She brightened. Joy was a tracking device of sorts.

Marks began writing again. "Okay, you were tracking Mr. Angelo because you felt concerned about his well-being."

She nodded. That was actually fairly accurate, even if less than twelve hours ago she'd thought he was a criminal. And twelve minutes ago, he'd been kissing her senseless.

"I caught up with him at a gas station and snuck him

out of the trunk. Shortly after that, Oscar Mooney called him on his WITSEC handler's phone. That's when we learned that Oscar—or his aid, this Mr. Smith—had overcome US Marshal Williams and kidnapped Mr. Angelo's daughter."

Autumn glanced over at the ambulance where Harriet sat with an ice pack to the back of her head and a cigarette dangling from her lips.

As Autumn continued to recite events, her gaze shifted intermittently to Devlin. He was free now. All threats to him had been neutralized. Would he go back to Sacramento? Chicago? Would he go back to being Aaron Somebody? He'd still have to testify, but he could be a paramedic again if he wanted.

And how would she finagle seeing him again? Perhaps something like a normal date? Would he want to see her, or would she be a reminder of the last twelve hours of misery he'd been through? The way he'd kissed her suggested he, too, wanted something more.

CHAPTER 12

*I*t was November tenth, but Devlin and Kimmy wore their Halloween costumes. Kimmy had missed Halloween, having slept through most of it, so Devlin and Autumn were throwing their own festive party for her.

When the doorbell rang, Kimmy raced to the front door in her Wonder Woman costume. "I got it! I got it!"

"Check the window before unlocking the door," Devlin called to her as he peeked through the kitchen window where he could see the front porch. Autumn stood at the door—she was always prompt.

"I know." Kimmy gave an exasperated sigh as she looked through the window. "It's Autumn!" She turned the lock and yanked the door open.

Kimmy grabbed Autumn's hand and pulled her inside before closing the door.

Autumn smiled. "Hey, Kimmy. Don't you look wonderful!"

"Did you wear yours?" Kimmy jumped in place, barely containing her bubbly excitement.

Autumn set down the tray of food she'd brought and twirled out of her cloak to reveal long, red boots, a fitted red, white, and blue outfit, and a gold lasso on her waist. Her streaked hair hung loose down her back.

Devlin's mouth hung open as he accidentally dropped the cork he'd just pulled from a bottle of wine. He fumbled to pick it up while Autumn carried her tray of food to the kitchen.

"Whoa!" Kimmy cried. "You look amazing!"

"You do look amazing," Devlin said, flustered he'd taken so long to find his voice to pay Autumn a compliment.

"Looking svelte yourself, Batman." Autumn winked, thumping a finger against his black breastplate.

Devlin set down the bottle of wine, leaned into Autumn, and gave her a brief kiss. He wanted to fully embrace her and kiss her more thoroughly, but Kimmy was watching them closely.

Kimmy, who, thanks to Autumn's heroics, wouldn't have to suffer a new identity or new home. Everyone who had been a threat to them was behind bars. Devlin didn't have to live in fear or in hiding anymore. He could be a paramedic again, though he doubted he would, because the shift work wasn't conducive to having the freedom to see Kimmy before and after school every day like he wanted.

He planned on keeping his name. He'd been Devlin Angelo for six years, and the two women who mattered most to him, who were with him tonight, knew him as such.

"Harriet stopped by."

"How is she?" Autumn asked.

"Back on duty and recovered from her concussion."

When Kimmy busied herself poking around the various food options—hot dogs dressed to look like mummies with mustard-yellow eyes, deviled eggs that looked like eyeballs, and a Jell-O brain mold—Devlin eased closer to Autumn.

"Thank you for doing this."

She smiled. "No little girl should miss Halloween. Besides, I'm looking forward to a Halloween dance party."

"Ah, yes. The dancing was Kimmy's idea."

"It'll be fun."

"You say that now, before you've seen me dance." Although he played reluctant, the thought of dancing with Autumn had his blood pumping.

"Dancing!" Kimmy exclaimed. She rushed to the home audio system and started playing "Monster Mash."

Devlin laughed.

"Is Joy here?" Autumn asked in a lowered voice.

"Somewhere close. I was hoping after Kimmy goes to bed, we could hold a ceremony for her and Bernard to help her move on."

Autumn nodded, then looked at Kimmy and back to Devlin. "Is this a date?"

He looked her up and down with a grin. "If so, that's one incredible first-date outfit." He leaned closer. "I'd like it to be the first of many dates. It's a little unconventional, but then so is everything about us so far."

Autumn's beaming smile lit up Devlin's world.

"Dance! Dance!" Kimmy spun circles in the living room, her Wonder Woman skirt twirling around her.

Devlin took Autumn's hand and led her to the open living room floor.

AFTER KIMMY HAD GONE to bed, Devlin arranged candles in a circle and had Autumn sit within it.

"This is cozy." Autumn crossed her legs and tucked her faux fur-lined cloak around her.

"Well, Joy certainly deserves a proper farewell. She's saved my life a few times." Devlin sat down in front of Autumn.

"Speaking of that night. I didn't want to say anything in front of Kimmy, but I thought I'd give you the wrap-up on Cesar Torres and the heroin. Joy's license-plate tip paid off, and Special Agent Marks caught up with Bernard's killer. I identified him, so you'll remain anonymous. The hitman only ever saw you with the top hat and fake gray beard, so he can't identify you."

He'd also closed the psychic business to prevent anyone from tracing him there and showing up looking for revenge on account of the heroin confiscated by the FBI.

"Joy told me," he said.

"Ah. Of course ,she did. I suppose there's no surprising a man who can talk to ghosts."

Devlin took Autumn's hand, leaned forward, and gave her the kiss he'd been wanting to give her since she'd shown up at his door tonight. "I'm surprised you're here. I'm surprised you're starting a relationship with a man with so much baggage, some of which is paranormal."

"I don't see baggage. I see a rough past overcome with perseverance. I see a father who'd do anything for his smart, adorable daughter. I see a man who's witty and wise." Autumn touched a hand to his cheek. "But you're going to be impossible to buy birthday gifts for if ghosts give away the secret."

Devlin grinned, looking into liquid gold eyes made magical in the candlelight. "My birthday is in March. If you join me for a candle-lit dinner, that's gift enough."

"I'd like that."

"Ready to say goodbye to Joy?"

"Ready."

~

ALMOST ONE YEAR LATER

AUTUMN FOLLOWED Kimmy to the next decorated house on Halloween night. All three of them wore angel costumes. Devlin's costume looked particularly scrumptious, owing to the revealing cut of his toga.

Now that Devlin's testimony had been given and Oscar's trial had ended with a guilty verdict, Devlin had been freed from his fear and freed from living in hiding. "Aunt" Harriet still came by for visits to see Kimmy.

Autumn walked along the side of the road as Kimmy ran up the sidewalk. When Devlin stood beside Autumn, she reached up and adjusted his halo.

"You may look like an angel, Mr. Angelo, but you bring out the devil in me."

He chuckled as he wrapped an arm around her waist. "Why, Mrs. Angelo, I believe we're all a bit of both."

Devlin was her angel, she knew. They'd saved each other last Halloween. Devlin had given her love, family, and a life she'd never known could be so wonderful. Rather than return to his medium work, Devlin helped Autumn solve her cases in instances where supernatural forces made themselves available for consultation. When she traveled, he stayed home with Kimmy, unless it coincided with a school break where they could all travel together.

Kimmy skipped past them, on to the next porch, where an enormous spiderweb and red glowing light awaited her.

Devlin took Autumn's hand as they walked to keep pace with the girl. "I was thinking about drawing you a nice bubble bath and pouring you a glass of wine, since you don't have to work tomorrow."

"I'd like that. But without the wine."

He gave her an inquisitive look.

"I should ask you how you feel about adding a fourth angel to our family."

Devlin's eyes went wide as a giddy grin spread across his face. He looked at her abdomen and back into her eyes. "Are you? Are we?"

Autumn laughed. "Yes. We're expecting."

Devlin picked her up and spun her in a circle. She wrapped her arms around his neck and gave him a tender kiss.

Autumn rested her head on his chest in contentment. "My angel."

<<<THE END>>>

***** QUICK NOTE FROM THE AUTHOR *****

READY FOR ANOTHER sweet and magical romantic suspense? There are so many delights to enjoy! Keep scrolling for the first chapter in the next book.

Romancing the Spirit

IN BOXED SETS

INDIVIDUAL BOOKS
Romancing the Spirit Series #1
Sadie's Spirit / Willow's Windfall
Cassie's Chase / Phoebe's Pharaoh
Vanessa's Valentine / Autumn's Angel
Romancing the Spirit Series #2
Carol's Christmas / Allison's Alibi
Gracelynn's Genie / Michelle's Miracle
Heather's Hero / Chloe's Cupid
Romancing the Spirit Series #3

Sabrina's Storm / Jenny's Justice
Stella's Star / Gigi's Gift
Phoenix's Phantom / Fiona's Freedom

THE CHRISTMAS COLLECTION

DEAR READER

Want to keep in touch?

If you enjoyed this book and want to know about future releases by CB Samet you can CLICK HERE to sign up for my mailing list! I promise I won't spam you. I only send an email when I have a new book released, giveaways, or special discounts. You can also unsubscribe at any time.

If you loved this book, kindly let others know by posing a brief comment on social media or leave a review where you purchased it so readers can find their next favorite romantic suspense series.

Even more ways to follow me below!

Thank you for reading,
CB Samet

CAROL'S CHRISTMAS

One night.

Two hearts.

Three spirits.

A new twist on a Christmas classic.

Dr. Carol Sullivan is a cold, bitter surgeon who focuses on the bottom line. She's distanced herself from friends, families, and even the love of her life. When the ghost of her former colleague visits, he promises a chance at salvation.

Over the course of the night, three ghosts visit Carol, and she reconsiders the choices she's made, and the person she's become. But can she truly make the difficult transformation or is compassion--and love--lost forever?

～

SAMPLE CHAPTER

"She's going to die." Tony Olsen paced the small office in the back of the pawnshop.

"Relax. Everybody dies, Tony." Burke took a drag off the cigarette that perpetually hung from his bottom lip. "I mean, look at the pair of us—a couple of nobody ghosts who don't want to move on."

Tony ran a hand through his gray hair. "But I've seen her death, Burke. Christmas morning. Bam!" He smacked his hands together. "Hit by a delivery truck. A truck!"

He'd watched the vision of Carol's death in slow motion. She walked toward the curb, distracted and not checking traffic. She stepped off into the road, and the truck that hit her didn't have time to slow down, or even swerve.

"There's a lot of tragedy in this world, Tony. She's lived to be forty-two, and that's a lot more than some people get."

Burke leaned back in his chair. The chair didn't move or squeak beneath his weight, and there was no noise even as he clumped his feet up onto the office desk.

"Besides," he continued, "from what you've told me about this woman, she don't got much of a life nowadays as it is."

Tony shoved his hands in his slacks—his Giorgio Armani suit pants. They were the very ones he'd been buried in when he'd died, five years earlier. Since his death, he'd been lingering as a spirit on earth, watching Carol Sullivan live the same life he'd had, making the same heartless, callous mistakes.

"Well, I'm partly to blame." Tony had never been kind to Carol. As a result of that—and other contributing factors from her past—she'd grown to become as cold and lonely as an iceberg, and drifting into an ever-melting, lifeless existence just the same.

"She can't even hear or see me," Tony continued. "How am I supposed to save her?"

Some living people had a gift—the ability to see and hear ghosts. The so-called mediums, however, were few and far between—and Carol wasn't one of them.

"She doesn't have any friends or family who can see ghosts. Without an intermediary, I can't reach out to her." Tony had been reduced to helplessly watching Carol ruin her life.

Burke pulled the cigarette out of his mouth and flicked nonexistent ashes off the glowing, orange tip. He stared at one of the walls of the pawnshop, where yellow paint was peeling from the plaster. Tony kept quiet. He recognized Burke's narrow-eyed gaze of contemplation.

Tony hadn't known Burke in life. He'd never have associated with a pawnshop owner. In death however, Burke had become his best friend. Tony wished he'd taken time to make friendships like this while he'd still been alive—but being a ghost was all about languishing in regret, wasn't it?

Burke scratched at his large belly.

"Save her, eh? Might be a way to … but not in the way you think."

"I'll try anything." Tony couldn't stomach the thought of a talented surgeon like Carol dying before she recognized the opportunity to turn her life around.

"You can make your case to the Christmas Spirits."

"The Christmas Spirits? They really exist?"

"Of course. Some spirits can be seen by whomever they choose at certain times of the year. The Christmas trio is already *real* busy this time of year, though. They're probably booked up. Some people start booking them a year in advance."

"They could help me help Carol?"

"They don't save lives. They save souls."

Tony's posture slumped. He wanted both for Carol—her life and her soul—and Christmas was only a week away. What were the chances his Christmas miracle could be worked into the busy schedules of the Christmas Spirits?

But he had to try—for Carol.

"So, is it like in the stories?" Tony asked. "The Christmas Spirits can save a soul in one night?" He sighed as he considered this. "They'd have to. She wouldn't have very long to live after that." He pressed the palms of his hands into his eyes, trying to block out the future image he'd seen of Carol getting hit by a truck on Christmas morning.

In his vision, she'd distractedly walked to the curb.

She'd stepped over the edge.

The end.

Burke shrugged, though his eyes looked at Tony with compassion.

"At least she'd have salvation. She can set things in motion to give her peace as a spirit. She wouldn't be lingering, like you—stuck wondering how to fix the cold-hearted deeds of her life."

"Okay. I'll do it. Where can I find the Christmas Spirits?"

"This close to Christmas? They oughta be at Michigan Avenue, under the Chicago Christmas tree."

<<<BUY CAROL'S CHRISTMAS TODAY>>>

OTHER BOOKS BY CB SAMET

Looking for more romantic suspense with more action and sizzle? How about with an urban fantasy twist? Check out my supernatural adventures...

The Shadow Guardians Trilogy

Urban fantasy Norse Mythology Adventure

Get *Raven's Flight, a prequel novella* for FREE. In my newsletter, you'll learn about me, special discounts, and new releases.

Raven's Flight, prequel novella

Raine Down, Book 1

Rosalyn's Run, novella

Storm Surge, Book 2

Anka's Orb, novella

Sky Fall, Book 3

Olympian Awakenings Trilogy

Urban fantasy Greek Mythology Adventure

Grab the prequel exclusively HERE.

Stone Hearts

Winds of Destiny

Flame and Shadow

∾

The Dr. Whyte Adventure Novels

Thriller Series

Black Gold

Whyte Knight

Gray Horizon

Love action/adventure and strong female leads in a fantasy world? Check out my other genre:

The Avant Champion Fantasy Series

The Avant Champion: Rising

Malakai: An Avant Champion Origin of Malos Story (prequel)

The Avant Champion: Honor

The Avant Champion: Ashes

Brothers' Bond: An Avant Champion Malakai Story

The Avant Champion: Conquest

Isabel: An Avant Champion novelette

The Avant Champion: Redeem

Follow Me

BOOKBUB

FACEBOOK

YOUTUBE

PINTEREST

INSTAGRAM

GOODREADS

CHIRP

TIKTOK